THE CASE OF THE

ECCENTRIC ELKHOUND

A Thousand Islands Doggy Inn Mystery

B.R. SNOW

Copyright © 2017 B.R. Snow

ISBN: 978-1-942691-13-6

Website: www.brsnow.net/

Twitter: @BernSnow

Facebook: facebook.com/bernsnow

Cover Design: Reggie Cullen

Cover Photo: James R. Miller

Other Books by B.R. Snow

The Thousand Islands Doggy Inn Mysteries

The Case of the Abandoned Aussie

The Case of the Brokenhearted Bulldog

The Case of the Caged Cockers

The Case of the Dapper Dandie Dinmont

The Damaged Po$$e Series

American Midnight

Larrikin Gene

Sneaker World

Summerman

The Duplicates

Other books

Divorce Hotel

Either Ore

To Dianne

Chapter 1

I stepped inside C's feeling like a kid on Christmas morning, caught a whiff of something that reminded me of Thanksgiving, and immediately knew that this Memorial Day would be one I'd always remember. I'd never been to the opening night of a new restaurant, and my anticipation, along with everyone else's, had been building over the past month as our official launch date approached.

We removed our coats and handed them to the hostess, and I caught my first good look at Josie's dress. I shook my head and laughed, realizing that soon every eye in the restaurant would be on her. We didn't dress up often, but when we did, Josie took it very seriously. When she heard me laugh, she turned and gave me a quizzical look.

"What's so funny?" Josie said.

"What happened to your dress?" I said.

"What do you mean what happened to it?" she said, glancing down, then over her shoulder.

"Did they run out of fabric?" I deadpanned.

"What on earth are you talking about?" she said, genuinely confused.

"There's no back," I said, laughing again.

"Oh, that," she said, relaxing. "I thought I might have spilled something on it already." She turned sideways and took a

1

look at herself in the floor length mirror near the entrance. "Is it too much?"

"Only for the men with bad hearts," I said, glancing around. "The place looks amazing."

We looked around at the polished hardwood floors, then up at the rotunda-style ceiling. A massive chandelier had been lovingly restored and was lit by a series of pin lights from several directions. It gave the main room a sense of elegance I hadn't believed possible when my mother first bought the rundown building several months ago, and we had decided to open C's. Our original plan was to open a restaurant primarily as a way to keep our good friend and housemate, Chef Claire, from leaving town. But as the renovations progressed, and we began to visualize what the place would look like, our excitement built and a sense of pride emerged.

"Can you believe we're part owners of this place?" I said, waving at several friends who were already sitting at their tables.

"No," Josie said, also waving. "And I think we've got a hit on our hands. Chef Claire said we're already booked solid for the next three weeks."

The place was indeed full, and we'd been forced to squeeze in a couple extra tables to accommodate some friends we wanted here to help us celebrate opening night. I spotted my mother holding court at a round table set for twelve in the small alcove she'd placed permanent dibs on. As soon as my mother had noticed the alcove, she'd taken over the responsibility of furnishing it. She'd found the table and chairs at an antique shop in Montreal along with an ornate rug and a couple of small tables and lamps. The area of the restaurant we now referred to as Mrs. C's Corner resembled a family dining room and I had to admit that my original fears that it would look out of place were unfounded. It looked fantastic, as did my mother. She waved at us, and I took my seat on her immediate left. Josie sat down next to me, leaned left, and gave Jackson, our local chief of police, a kiss on the cheek.

"Hello, darling," my mother said. "You look wonderful. Is that new?"

"Hi, Mom," I said, giving her a hug. "No, I've had this awhile. I just never seem to get a chance to wear it."

"That's because you insist on spending your evenings at home wearing sweatpants," she said, pouring two glasses of champagne.

"Let's not go there tonight, Mom," I said, handing one of the glasses to Josie.

"Gorgeous dress, Josie," my mother said.

"Thanks, Mrs. C."

I looked around the table and smiled and waved at Jackson, our chief of police, who was sitting next to our local medical examiner, Freddie. Next to him was Sammy and Jill, our two primary staff members, who were very much in love with each other as well as all our dogs. We'd asked our two summer interns to keep an eye on things at the Inn tonight since there was no way we would have allowed Sammy and Jill to miss the opening.

On my mom's immediate right was Howard Sands, the Mayor of Clay Bay and someone I'd known since I was a little girl. I gave him a small wave, and a smile then glanced around the rest of the table. I didn't know the other four people and waited for my mother to handle the introductions.

"Darling, I don't believe you know Jimmy," my mother said. "Jimmy, I'd like you to meet my daughter Suzy. And sitting next to her is Josie. They run the Thousand Islands Doggy Inn you've heard so much about."

"It's nice to meet you, ladies," he said, "I'm Jimmy Calducci."

He was wearing a shiny dark blue suit and periwinkle tie, and his gray hair was slicked back. My mother was right; I'd never met him, but his name rang a bell. Before I had time to ponder, Calducci continued with the introductions.

"This is my wife, Dot. If you want to talk with her I suggest you try to do it early in the evening," Calducci said with a laugh.

"Right back at you, dear," Dot said, not even bothering to make eye contact with her husband.

"Next to her is Pee Wee. And next to him is Franny. They both work for me," he said, sitting back in his chair. "So you're the two dog folks you're mother has told me so much about."

"I wouldn't believe too much of what she tells you, Jimmy. She's a drinker."

"Funny, darling."

Jimmy thought it was, and he laughed long and hard. While he did, I took a few moments to check out the other three strangers. Calducci's wife was around my mom's age and like my mother was doing a good job of beating back the aging process. She seemed to have a small smile frozen in place and was making short work of her champagne. Pee Wee, on her immediate right, must have been given his name by someone trying to be clever. He was huge with a thick neck that was threatening to disappear into his shoulders. It appeared he wasn't a fan of and chitchat, and he constantly scanned the restaurant as if it was a job assignment. Next to him was an attractive woman somewhere in her thirties Calducci had introduced as Franny. She gave me a small smile, but it had an edge to it, and her eyes were half-closed. I decided the sleepy look was an affectation since it was obvious she wasn't missing anything happening in the restaurant.

"I'm a big dog guy myself," Calducci said. "I just got a beautiful Elkhound puppy a couple of months ago."

"Oh, I love those," Josie said. "They have that tail that curls up all the way up."

"They're the national dog of Norway, right?" I said.

"That's the one," Calducci said, chuckling. "He's beautiful and growing fast, but I gotta say he's a real handful."

"He's an idiot," Dot said, draining her champagne and holding out her glass for Pee Wee to refill. "I'm sure he gets that from his master."

Josie and I both did our best not to glare at Calducci's wife. We'd never met a stupid dog, but we'd certainly met a lot of stupid owners.

"He's not an idiot, my dear," Calducci said, his voice low and tempered. "Oslo is just a bit eccentric."

Dot scoffed at her husband's response and took a gulp of champagne. But the odd smile remained frozen on her face.

"Oslo?" I said. "What a cool name."

"Thanks," Calducci said, then turned to the mayor sitting to his left. "So, they elected you mayor, Howard?"

"Yeah," Howard said, reluctantly acknowledging Calducci. "You sound surprised."

"Actually, shock would be more like it," Calducci said, laughing. "But I guess every dog has its day, right? You remember that time I stuffed you in your school locker?"

"Yeah, sure I remember, Jimmy," Howard said, staring off into the distance.

"Did you grow up around here, Mr. Calducci?" I said.

"Early on. I left when I was twelve," Calducci said.

"Left? If I remember correctly," Howard said. "Wasn't it more like you were sent away?"

Calducci flinched, and my mother leaned forward and placed a hand on the mayor's arm.

"Jimmy and I go way back, darling," my mother said. "And after he left the area, we've managed to stay in touch all these years. Isn't that right, Jimmy?"

"It certainly is," Calducci said, raising his glass and toasting my mother.

"Why does his name sound so familiar?" Josie whispered.

"I don't know," I whispered back. "And it's driving me crazy."

Our waitress arrived carrying a stack of menus.

"Good evening, folks," she said. "How are you doing tonight?"

"We're great, Cynthia," my mother said. "Is everything going well so far?"

"It's fantastic, Mrs. C.," the waitress said. "It's a little hectic in the kitchen, but that's to be expected."

"How's Chef Claire holding up?" I said.

"She's amazing. And all the staff just loves her. Chef Claire said to tell you that she'll come out to say hi as soon as she gets a chance."

"Wonderful," my mother said, accepting one of the menus.

I also took one of the menus and smiled as the waitress started to hand one to Josie.

"Thanks, but I won't need one of those," Josie said, shaking her head.

It was true. She didn't. Josie had spent the last two weeks memorizing the menu and had gone through a dozen different order combinations before finally deciding on what she'd be having tonight.

"You're Josie, right?" the waitress said, smiling.

"Yeah?"

"Chef Claire said you probably wouldn't need a menu," the waitress said. "She said you know it better than she does."

"Josie is a bit of a menu aficionado," I said, laughing.

Everyone at the table who knew Josie laughed. The Calducci clan looked on with bemused expressions.

"I'll be back in a few minutes to take your orders," the waitress said, then strolled off.

"Have you changed your mind again about what you're going to have?" I said.

"No," Josie said. "I think I've got it perfected. I'm going to start with a bowl of the Thai red curry soup, followed by the Caprese salad, then the Josie cut prime rib with the gruyere scalloped potatoes and the mushroom medley."

"The Josie cut?" Calducci's wife said, raising an eyebrow.

"We have three different cuts of the prime rib," I said. "The smallest one is named The Mrs. C. The regular cut is The Suzy. And for the truly adventurous, there's The Josie."

I spread my thumb and index finger about two inches apart to demonstrate.

"Are you really going to eat all that food?" Calducci said, chuckling, yet sounding surprised.

"You bet she is," Jackson said.

"Just don't get too close when's she holding a knife and fork and you'll be fine, Mr. Calducci," I said, laughing.

"And whatever you do, never sneak up behind her when she's eating," Jackson said.

"Funny," Josie said, unfolding her napkin.

She knocked her fork off the table and bent down to pick it up. Seconds later she popped up and placed the fork on the table and sat back in her chair. I noticed the odd look on her face and leaned closer to her.

"What?" I whispered.

"I just happened to see something under the table," she whispered.

"Please don't tell me you saw a rat," I whispered. "That's all we need on opening night."

"No, nothing like that. It was Pee Wee's hand."

"His hand? Where?" I whispered.

"On Calducci's wife's leg."

"Like a fatherly pat on the knee?" I whispered.

"More like a dirty uncle squeeze," she whispered into her napkin.

"On her thigh?"

"I guess it could still be considered part of the thigh," Josie whispered, then wiped her mouth with the napkin.

"That explains the goofy smile she's had on her face since we sat down," I said, slightly louder.

"Knock it off," my mother whispered as she glared at us. "It's not ladylike to whisper at the table."

"You're whispering," I said to my mother.

"Be that as it may, darling," my mother said, taking a sip of champagne and leaning closer. "What's so important that you two need to whisper like a couple of five-year-olds?"

"Pee Wee's playing squeeze the thigh with Dot under the table," I whispered into her ear, sneaking a glance at Calducci who remained oblivious to what was happening right under his nose.

"Really?" my mother whispered. "I was wondering why she seemed so happy tonight. She's usually a miserable human being."

"Who is this Calducci guy, Mom?" I whispered. "His name sounds familiar, and I don't know why. It's driving me crazy."

"We'll have that conversation later," my mother said, sitting upright in her chair. "Trust me, darling. It's not one we want to have over dinner."

Chapter 2

By the time eleven o'clock rolled around, we'd said goodbye to nearly everyone who'd come to opening night and headed for the lounge where Chef Claire was already waiting for us. We paused near the door to say goodbye to the Calducci clan who were waiting for their coats. They, like the rest of us, were stuffed and moving slowly. Mrs. Calducci was being held upright by Pee Wee who had his arm around her waist. I'd lost track of how many glasses of champagne she'd had, but I knew if Pee Wee let go, Calducci's wife would drop like a rock. Jimmy ignored his wife as he slipped his coat on and hugged my mother.

"What a meal," he gushed. "What a restaurant. Just incredible."

"Thanks, Jimmy," my mother said. "I'm so glad you enjoyed it. And thanks again for coming."

"I wouldn't have missed it," Calducci said. "And if the restaurant is ever in need of my services, you be sure and let me know."

"You'll be the first person we call, Jimmy," my mother said.

"You sure you can't make it tomorrow," Calducci said. "It should be a lot of fun."

"Oh, I wish I could, Jimmy," my mother said, turning on the charm. "But we have some restaurant business to take care of. I'm sure you understand."

"Okay. But you're coming the next time we take the houseboat out," Calducci said. "And I won't take no for an answer."

"You got it, Jimmy," my mother said, smiling as she gave him a peck on the cheek. "Good night all. Drive safe."

Franny, the woman with the narrow eyes, pushed the front door open, scanned the immediate area outside, then nodded at Calducci. He nodded at Pee Wee who then helped Dot out the door then gave us a small wave as they departed. Franny waited until everyone was outside then nodded at us and mumbled a quick thank you just before the door closed behind her.

We walked into the lounge and found Chef Claire sitting on one of the couches sipping wine and reviewing a huge stack of receipts. I sat down next to her and gave her a long hug.

"Congratulations," I said. "Everyone is raving about the place."

"Thanks, Suzy," Chef Claire said as tears welled in her eyes.

"What's the matter?" I said.

"I'm just so happy," Chef Claire said. "I can't believe the renovations are finally done, and we've opened. And the place looks beautiful."

Josie sat down on the other side of Chef Claire. My mother, along with Jackson and Freddie, sat down on a couch directly across from us. Everyone congratulated Chef Claire, and she modestly accepted their well wishes and thanks.

"Can I get you guys an after dinner drink?" Chef Claire said.

Everyone, except Josie, shook their heads.

"Alka-Seltzer on the rocks for me, please," Josie said, pressing a hand against her chest. "Man, I'm such a little piggy."

"You'll get no argument from me," I said, shaking my head. "But I wasn't quite sure until I watched you polish off that third soufflé."

"Funny," Josie said, rubbing her stomach. "Hey, it was obvious Dot wasn't going to eat it, and there was no way I was going to let it go to waste."

"Calducci's wife was totally hammered by eight o'clock," I said.

"She's always hammered, darling," my mother said.

"Man, she can really put the champagne away," I said.

"My guess is that she has the same skillset when it comes to bourbon and scotch," Josie said.

"Okay, Mom, now that they're gone, how about telling me the story?" I said. "Why is this guy's name so familiar?"

Jackson and Freddie laughed. I stared at them, then looked at my mother.

"It's basically like I told you earlier, darling. Jimmy grew up in the area, and we hung out when we were kids. We were buddies."

Jackson laughed again, and my mother glared at him.

"As long as you weren't partners in crime, Mrs. C.," Jackson said.

"Knock it off, Jackson," my mother said. "Those are just a bunch of unfounded rumors."

"Right," Jackson said. "And I'm a ballerina."

"Would you two mind getting to the point?" I said.

"Think it through, Suzy," Jackson said, leaning forward. "Slicked back hair, shiny suit, the way he smiles at you while staring a hole in your head. Travels around with a bodyguard."

"He's a criminal?" I said.

"No, darling, he's not a criminal," my mother said, glaring at Jackson.

"*Calducci?*" Jackson said, then let his comment hang in the air.

"The mob?" I said, my eyes wide. "Mom, are you saying Calducci is a mafia guy?"

"Of course not, darling," my mother said. "That's what Jackson is saying. Jimmy's not even Italian."

"Calducci sure sounds Italian to me," Freddie said.

"He changed his last name after he left town," my mother said.

"That's right," Jackson said. "I can't even remember what his original name was."

"Fingerslit," my mother said quietly.

"That's it," Jackson said, laughing. "Little Jimmy Fingerslit."

"I probably would have changed it, too," Josie said, frowning. "Fingerslit. Not good."

"But why did he change it to an Italian name?" I said to my mother.

"I guess it helped him fit in better with his new community," my mother said.

"I'm sure it did," Jackson said, laughing again.

"Jackson, you've been watching too many movies," my mother said. "And all you're doing is helping perpetuate a myth about the Italian community."

"Sorry to disagree with you, Mrs. C.," Jackson said. "And while I'd never do anything that might offend my many Italian friends when the shoe fits, right? Calducci is on the radar of every law enforcement agency on both sides of the River, and you know it."

"Perhaps," my mother said. "But Jimmy is a businessman who runs many legitimate companies."

"Name one," Jackson said.

"Well, for starters, one of his businesses is a restaurant supply company that specializes in meats and cheeses," my mother said. "And weren't you raving earlier this evening about the mozzarella in the Caprese?"

"Actually, Mrs. C.," Chef Claire said. "I make that mozzarella in-house."

"Really?" my mother said, raising an eyebrow at Chef Claire. "Well then, bravo, my dear."

"Will you forget the mozzarella?" I said, my voice rising.

"I'll never be able to forget it," Josie deadpanned. "It's life-affirming."

"Mom, are you saying that some of the stuff we're using in the restaurant is supplied by the Mob?"

"No," my mother said. "Not technically. I'm pretty sure the meat and cheese operation is legitimate."

"But you're not positive?" I said, glaring at her.

"Tomato, tomahto, darling."

"Morrie the Meat Guy?" Chef Claire said. "You mean to tell me that nice old man works for this guy Calducci and is mobbed up?"

"No, of course not," my mother said, now completely playing defense and not liking it one bit. "Morrie doesn't work for him, per se. Jimmy's role is more of an *overseer*."

"Overseer as in the guy who holds a gun against your head while looking over your shoulder," Jackson said.

"Knock it off, Jackson," my mother said.

"I can't believe you brought a mob guy into our new restaurant," I said.

16

"I did no such thing, darling. Just try to tell me that the meat and cheese products aren't some of the best you've ever tasted. And that whole mob thing is just an old wives' tale."

"It's just such a pity that most of them don't live long enough to tell it," Jackson said, laughing.

"You're not funny, Jackson," my mother said.

"No, I think you've gotta give him credit for that one, Mrs. C.," Josie said, nodding. "That was good."

"Thanks, Josie," Jackson said.

"Geez, Mom," I said. "What are you doing hanging around this guy?"

"I already told you," my mother said. "And I must say, darling, as usual, you're overreacting. We're simply old friends, and when he told me was going to be in town for Memorial Day, I invited him to join us for dinner."

"Well, if Jimmy Calducci is in town, you can bet somebody is about to be in a world of hurt," Jackson said.

"Jackson, don't you have some parking tickets to write?" my mother said, again glaring at our chief of police.

"Not until morning, Mrs. C.," Jackson said, grinning. "All I'm saying is that when Calducci is around, trouble seems to follow close behind."

"He was just here for the food," my mother said. "And he was also nice enough to invite all of us out on his houseboat tomorrow as his guest. Based on this conversation, I'm glad I had the foresight to decline his generous offer."

"You didn't feel like spending the day on the River with him and his two goons?" Jackson said, laughing.

"You should probably let it go, Jackson," I said, unable to miss the look on my mother's face. Then I paused and thought about his comment. "*Two* goons?"

"Yeah, Pee Wee, the guy with no neck, and Franny," Jackson said.

"The sleepy one with the narrow eyes?" I said, frowning.

"Don't let that fool you," Jackson said. "She's one of the top shooters around."

"A hit woman? She actually shoots people for money?" I said, staring at him in disbelief.

"Yeah, I'm sure Fatal Franny does it for money. Or when she's just in a bad mood, and you happen to look at her the wrong way," Jackson said.

"Fatal Franny?" I whispered.

"Kinda catchy, huh?" Jackson said.

"Mom, I don't want those people hanging around the restaurant," I said.

"Relax, darling," my mother said. "They don't even live in the area. Besides, Jimmy would never do anything that might embarrass me."

"You mean like shoot somebody in the parking lot?" I said.

"Drop it, darling," my mother said. "You've made your point, and you're starting to repeat yourself."

"Geez, Mom," I said, shaking my head at her. "I'm really sorry about that. I just didn't know that I'd be sharing opening night dinner with a mobster."

"Don't forget, darling," my mother said, giving me a crocodile smile. "You also spent the evening with your best friends and me. Not to mention our mayor."

"Yeah, I was wondering about that, Mrs. C.," Jackson said. "What's the history between Howard and Calducci? I picked up on some bad blood between them."

"Yes," my mother said, nodding. "They've never been able to get past it. Howard used to date Jimmy's wife, Dot. And they were quite an item for a couple of years. Then Jimmy came back into town one summer and swept Dot off her feet. Howard never forgave him."

"The way she looked by the end of the night," Jackson said. "I'd say Howard might have dodged a bullet there."

"She's had a tough go of things," my mother said. "And the booze certainly isn't helping. She still looks great, but you should have seen her back in the day. She could have almost rivaled Josie in the looks department."

"Why thanks, Mrs. C.," Josie said, beaming. "You're so sweet."

"You're welcome, dear," my mother said, glaring at me. "It's nice to see that someone notices."

"Geez, Mom," I said, shaking my head. "All right. You win. I'm sorry I hurt your feelings."

"Apology accepted, darling," my mother said, settling back into the couch. "But I must admit that those two creatures Jimmy has working for him were almost enough to put me off my food. The one called Pee Wee looks like he could explode at any minute. He seems incredibly unstable."

"I don't know Mrs. C.," Josie deadpanned. "From what I saw, it looked like he had a pretty good grip on things most of the evening."

I snorted and laughed until my mother cut it short with a glare.

"Don't be disgusting, Josie," my mother snapped.

"Hey, don't look at me," she said. "My hands were on the table the whole time."

Chapter 3

I slowed down when we left the main shipping channel, and we waved at a tour boat that was just departing from Boldt Castle, one of the prime tourist attractions in the area. Captain and Chloe recognized the castle as we cruised past it, and they began pacing back and forth and excitedly wagging their tails.

"They know where we're going," Josie said, nodding her head at the dogs.

"They're both way too smart," I said, laughing. "You guys want to go for a swim?"

Chloe barked once, and Captain sat down in front of Josie and placed a massive paw on her leg.

"Hold your horses," Josie said, rubbing the Newfie's head, which, like the rest of him, seemed to be getting bigger by the day.

We'd spent the day at the Inn dealing with many of the same issues we did most weekends during the summer. And this year's Memorial Day looked like it wouldn't be any different. A couple of lost dogs were dropped off at the Inn, then eventually reunited with their concerned owners. Two other dogs had helped themselves to their family's barbecue when no one was looking and eaten several hamburgers stuffed with chopped onions. After the owner arrived with both dogs, he eventually fessed up after persistent questioning from Josie, that both Labs had also eaten an unattended pot of grilled onions. Josie and Sammy had induced vomiting in both dogs, flushed their stomachs, and gave both of them a bath to help prevent external infection. After keeping a close eye on the dogs for most of the afternoon, they were released, and they left the Inn happily wagging their tails while their embarrassed owner left with his tail tucked between his legs.

We were still trying to adjust to the fact that Chef Claire wasn't often around during dinner. And now that the restaurant was open, we'd be seeing even less of her. After a dinner of leftover lasagna, we'd decided to take the dogs out on the boat and head to the Lake of the Isles. The early evening air was warm, but I knew the water was still freezing. And since the water in the Lake of the Isles was shallower, it tended to warm up before other sections of the River. I knew the dogs really didn't care too much about the water temperature, but, on their behalf, I did.

Especially since they'd be shaking themselves off all over me when they got out.

The area of the St. Lawrence known as the Lake of the Isles was quiet despite the holiday weekend. Most boaters had already headed home to have dinner and get ready for their evening activities, and the surface of the water was like glass. Just before I could comment on how the water skiers were missing out on perfect conditions, I spotted a woman in a wetsuit executing a perfect slalom run at a high rate of speed. Then she let her weight get too far forward, caught the tip of her ski in the wake, and catapulted face-first into the water.

"Ouch," Josie said. "That's gotta hurt."

"Yeah, it does," I said, remembering my own experience with the dreaded *tip catch* when I was younger. "But she's laughing, so she must be okay."

We watched the woman climb into the boat, and then it sped off leaving us and the setting sun by ourselves.

"I still don't understand why this place is called a lake," Josie said, opening a fresh bag of bite-sized Snickers.

"Josie, you do this every time we come here," I said, grabbing a small handful from the bag. "Let's not have this conversation again."

"It's technically still part of the River," she said. "And a lake is a body of water completely surrounded by land, not just on three sides. Why isn't it called a bay, or maybe an inlet?"

"It's a mystery all right," I said, exhaling as I slowed, then turned the boat off to drift. "You guys ready for a swim?"

Captain, closely followed by Chloe, launched himself off the back of the transom and started to powerfully swim away from the boat. Chloe did her best to keep up, but Captain was in his element. After a couple of minutes, Josie whistled loudly, and Captain turned and started back toward the boat. Josie tossed a handful of tennis balls in the water, and both dogs made a beeline for them.

"Watch this," Josie said, laughing.

Captain, despite Chloe's best efforts, ended up with all four balls in his mouth and he swam back to the boat with what looked like an enormous yellow grin. Chloe wasn't happy, and she playfully nipped at Captain's ear as they approached. Captain finally agreed to drop one of the balls and Chloe snatched it out of the water and raced back to the boat. We repeated the water version of fetch several times until both dogs were breathing heavily then helped both of them back onto the boat, getting soaked in the process. Then we got drenched when both dogs shook the water off.

"Wow," Josie said, shivering. "That water is still freezing."

"You know, when I was a kid, I wouldn't have thought twice about going in the water on Memorial Day," I said.

"You mean before you were old enough to know any better?"

"Exactly," I said, laughing. "Now I understand why my mother always refused to go in this time of the year."

Josie grabbed two towels, tossed me one, and we both rubbed them vigorously over the dogs.

"Okay, Chloe," I said, standing up to examine my work. "You can air dry on the way home."

I started the boat, and we retraced our route on the way out. I spotted another boat off in the distance, and it soon became clear that it was a houseboat. I nudged Josie and pointed at it.

"You don't think that's our friendly mobster's houseboat, do you?" Josie said.

"We'll know soon enough," I said. "Is that a dog running around the outside deck?"

Josie grabbed a pair of binoculars and looked through them.

"It certainly is," Josie said. "And unless I'm mistaken, that is definitely an Elkhound. Probably around six months old. Beautiful dog. What did Calducci say his name was?"

"Oslo," I said, slowing down as we approached the houseboat that appeared to be drifting. "We need to stop and say hello, or my mother will kill me for being rude."

I idled up to the houseboat, then turned the boat off. Josie tied ours to the houseboat, and the Elkhound trotted over and accepted a head scratch from Josie as it kept a wary eye on Captain and Chloe who were both glancing up at Oslo. The dog had a gorgeous gray and silver coat and was playful. I didn't have much experience with the breed but knew that they had a reputation for being brave and strong-willed, and extremely loyal. I watched the dog trot back and forth along the railing of the houseboat, then the Elkhound lost his balance and stumbled before catching himself. It resumed its bizarre trot around the deck of the houseboat that included several wheelies and head shakes. Then it started making a sound somewhere between a howl and a whine.

"Well," I said, chuckling at the dog's strange behavior. "Calducci did say the dog was eccentric."

"No," Josie said, watching the dog's movements closely. "That's not normal. I think something's wrong with him."

"Yeah, his owner is a gangster," I said, grinning.

"No, Suzy," Josie said. "I'm serious. There's definitely something wrong with him. I need to get him back to the Inn and take a look."

Knowing it was useless trying to argue with her when it came to her instincts as a veterinarian, I nodded and climbed aboard the houseboat. I glanced around the impressive top-of-the-line vessel.

"Great boat. Well, we better make sure we have permission before we take Oslo anywhere. I'm not stealing a mobster's dog," I said. "Chloe, stay."

Chloe barked once, but sat down and stayed put. Josie gave Captain the same command, then she joined me on the houseboat. Oslo trotted over and seemed to be listing toward one side. Then the dog started running in a circle, then stopped. He wagged his tail, then trotted away shaking his head.

"You're right," I said. "There's definitely something wrong with him. Let's go find, Mr. Calducci."

We approached a double glass door that led down into the galley and living quarters. The blinds inside were closed, and Josie knocked on the glass. When we didn't get any response, she knocked louder.

"What do you think?" Josie said. "I'd hate to just walk in on them."

"Yeah," I said, unsuccessfully trying to peer inside. "Give it one more."

Josie knocked on the glass again, but we still didn't get a response.

"They're probably taking a nap," I said. "But so be it. We're not taking Calducci's dog without permission. C'mon."

I slid the glass doors open and pushed the curtains back. We walked down a small set of steps directly into what was the living area. We glanced around, found the ornately furnished area empty, then Josie pointed at a closed door I assumed led to the master suite.

We knocked, then slid open the wood door and stood frozen in the doorway.

"Oh, no," Josie said. "Not another one."

"People are going to start avoiding us like the plague," I said, staring at the bed.

Jimmy Calducci, devoid of any visible wounds, lay on his back looking up at the ceiling with a vacant stare. Josie slowly made her way to the edge of the bed and checked for a pulse. Moments later, she looked at me with watery eyes and shook her head.

"Geez, the poor guy," I said, shaking my head. "I don't see any injuries or blood."

"No, me neither," Josie said. "Maybe he had a heart attack."

"Yeah, maybe," I said, my mind already racing. "I wonder where his wife and the rest of his gang are."

"Please, don't start, Suzy," Josie said, heading for the stairs that led back to fresh air.

27

"I don't know what you're talking about," I said, following her up the stairs.

On deck, I checked to make sure Captain and Chloe were still staying put. Then I grabbed my phone and dialed. Josie sat down in a deck chair deep in thought. I sat next to her and put my phone on speaker.

"This is Jackson."

"Hey, it's me."

"Hi, Suzy. What's shaking?"

"At the moment, my hands," I said.

"You lost me," Jackson said.

"Do you remember when you said last night that if Jimmy Calducci is in town, you can bet somebody is about to be in a world of hurt?"

"Yeah," Jackson said, warily.

"Well, you were right," I said.

"Aaahh. Really?" Jackson said, exhaling loudly. "Sometimes I hate being right. Who is it?"

"It's Calducci," I whispered.

"What? Is he dead?"

"Very," Josie said. "Hey, Jackson."

"Hi, Josie," Jackson said. "Are you okay?"

"I've been better," she said.

"Where's the body?" Jackson said.

"On his houseboat. Right near the entrance to Lake of the Isles," I said.

"And you just happened to stumble onto him?"

"Yeah. Pretty much," I said. "We'll wait here for you."

"Okay," he said. "There go my dinner plans."

"Sorry to do that to you, Jackson," I said. "Tell you what. Just call Chef Claire and ask her to add one more to our takeout order. Swing by the house after you finish up here, and it'll be waiting for you."

"Since when did you decide to start offering takeout?" Jackson said.

"We don't," I said. "It's just one of the perks of ownership."

"Good perk," Jackson said. "Okay, let me track down Freddie, and we'll be there as soon as we can. Don't touch anything."

I ended the call and slid my phone back in my pocket. Josie called Oslo, and the dog approached and sat patiently as Josie began gently examining the dog. The dog nudged her with his nose then licked her hand.

"He knows you're trying to help him," I said, staring at the dog.

"Yeah," Josie said, rubbing the dog's head. "Let's hope I'm not too late."

Chapter 4

We waited out the next half-hour in relative silence until Jackson and Freddie arrived. Josie helped them secure the police boat to Calducci's then they both climbed aboard the houseboat. Given the circumstances, our greeting was brief and all business. They followed us below deck to where the body was then Josie and I said our goodbyes. After explaining why we were taking Calducci's dog with us, we headed for home just before sunset and went directly to the Inn after we'd docked.

I followed Josie into one of the exam rooms, and she gently placed Oslo on a table. The dog, while still shaking its head and emitting the combination howl and whine sound that broke my heart, was relatively calm as Josie conducted her initial examination. I watched as she moved her index finger back and forth in front of the dog's face. I certainly wasn't a vet by any means, but the dog's eyes seemed to be having some difficulty following Josie's movements.

"What do you think?" I said, stroking the dog's thick fur.

"My first guess is that it's something neurological," Josie said. "There's no sign of a head fracture or any trauma. And he certainly looks like he's been well-cared for. I'm not ruling out hydrocephalus, but I'd expect to be seeing some swelling of the head."

"That's excessive fluids collecting inside the brain, right?" I said.

"Yeah, it's similar to water on the knee or elbow," Josie said. "Except this time, we're dealing with the brain. But I don't think that's it. I'm going to need to get some pictures."

"Brain tumor?" I whispered.

"Maybe," Josie said, glancing up at me. "I'm going to need your help, Suzy. So try and hold it together."

I blinked back the tears and nodded.

"Should we call Jill and have her come in?" I said.

"I think her and Sammy are out of town tonight," Josie said. "I can handle the anesthesiology, but I'll need some help from you if we have to do surgery. Better put on some scrubs."

I nodded and went to change clothes. A few minutes later, I joined Josie in the back of the Inn where she already had the sedated Oslo stretched out and ready for his MRI. Several people around town, including my mother, were baffled when they'd heard we had purchased an MRI scanner to be used exclusively on animals. After searching for months, we'd found a refurbished scanner that met all our needs. Even used, it still cost a small fortune, but our technology now rivaled that of the major veterinary operations found in major cities. And we regularly provided MRIs for other vets within a hundred mile radius who didn't have our resources and weren't able to afford what many considered a luxury.

But for us, it was just one more line item in the cost of doing business.

We'd recently done a presentation to the Town Council about the Inn's capabilities and our plans for expansion in both our capacity and overall range of services. Most of the Council members had been impressed by what we'd told them, but the mayor had challenged us with a comment about how the health and medical services available to dogs rivaled, and often exceeded, those available to residents at our local hospital.

Josie had listened closely to the mayor, then deadpanned, "Whose fault is that, Howard?"

Howard had turned bright red and quickly adjourned the meeting.

I smiled at the memory as I watched Josie handle the procedure and the young dog with a quiet, professional efficiency. She asked me to keep a close eye on the sedated Oslo while she headed off to examine the results of the MRI. When she returned, Josie had a blank look on her face I knew meant bad news.

"It's a tumor, isn't it?" I said.

"Yeah," Josie said, rubbing her forehead. "And it's in an area that would explain why he's showing a lot of those symptoms.

"But he's so young," I said. "He's barely done being a puppy."

"Yeah, it's unusual," Josie said. "But it does happen in younger dogs. It could be a simple case of bad genes."

"What are the odds it cancerous?" I said.

"I'm hoping they're low because he's so young, and it looks like we might have caught it early," Josie said. "But we won't be able to confirm that until we can get a biopsy done."

"Then should we wait until that's done before you do the surgery?" I said.

"That's the question I've been asking myself for the past hour. But I think that whatever is in there is pretty aggressive and is going to have to be removed at some point. So my instincts are telling me to go in now and take it out. And if the biopsy confirms cancer, we can follow up with chemo or radiation later on."

"Can you remove it without doing any more damage?" I said.

"I hope so," she whispered. "But I can't be sure until I get inside and a get a good look at what we're dealing with."

"Okay, then let's get started," I said, then noticed the look on Josie's face. "What is it?"

"I've never done surgery on a dog without their owner's permission," she said.

"I don't think that's going to be possible, Josie."

"I meant Calducci's wife," Josie said.

"I imagine Dot has other things she's dealing with at the moment," I said. "And wasn't she the one who called Oslo an idiot?"

"Yes, she was," Josie said.

"Well, I doubt if she is going to have a strong opinion either way as long as we don't ask her to pay for it."

"Yeah, I know," she said. "It just seems strange. But if Oslo doesn't make it, I'm going to have to do some serious explaining."

"If you don't do it, he's going to die, right?" I said.

"Eventually, yes," Josie said.

"And he'll be in increasing pain and discomfort as the tumor grows, right?" I said.

"Yeah."

"Then it's settled, isn't it?" I said.

Josie thought about it for several seconds, before nodding at me.

"It is," she said. "What's best for the dog always comes first."

"It's really risky surgery," I said.

"I thought you were just trying to talk me into it," Josie said, managing a small laugh.

"Yeah, I guess I was," I said, smiling nervously. "Never mind."

"Okay, are you ready?" she said, lifting the sedated dog in her arms. "I set the operating area up while I was waiting for the MRI results."

I followed her and spent the next two hours helping her keep an eye on the machines that were monitoring Oslo's vital signs as well as handle other tasks she gave me. I followed her instructions the best I could, and she did everything possible to avoid using medical jargon I wouldn't understand. I was fascinated by her precision, and when she was finally able to remove the small object, I exhaled loudly.

"Okay," Josie said, taking a final look at her work. "That's the best I can do. Let's hope it's enough."

"Amazing," I said.

"You did a good job," she said, chuckling. "You didn't faint or throw up once."

"Funny," I said, watching her efficiently stitch the wound closed. "I guess that's why they make you spend all those years in vet school, huh?"

"Yup," she said, stepping back from the table and removing her latex gloves. "He's going to need constant monitoring for a day or two."

"You want me to take the first shift?"

"No," Josie said. "I need to be here when he comes out of the anesthesia. But if you want to relieve me in about six hours, that would be great."

"You got it," I said, starting to walk away before stopping and looking back at her. "Josie?"

"Yeah."

"Thank you."

"For what?"

"Just for being you," I said.

"It's not like I have much choice, Suzy," she said, laughing. "Who else am I going to be?"

"Yeah, I guess you've got a good point there."

.

Chapter 5

After I had delivered Josie's dinner to her, I settled in with Chloe and Captain in the living room with designs on a nap before it was time to head back down to the Inn and relieve Josie. But my plans were interrupted when Chef Claire arrived home from the restaurant around eleven, trailed by Jackson and Freddie. The guys joined me in the living room for a glass of wine while Chef Claire headed off to take a shower to rinse off, as she called it, twelve hours of restaurant.

I glanced back and forth between them and waited for the update on Calducci. Jackson was the first one to catch the meaning behind my expression and went first.

"Well, I finally managed to get hold of the wife. According to her, she and Pee Wee spent the day shopping on the Canadian side," he said.

"Has Canadian Immigration confirmed they came across the border?" I said, sliding further down the couch to make room for Chloe.

"Dot said they went by boat and didn't bother to check in when they docked in Kingston," Jackson said.

I nodded, not surprised by that piece of information. Although boaters were expected to check in with local immigration officials when they came ashore, many didn't comply since they considered it an unnecessary annoyance.

"If they were shopping, a quick check of credit card activity would help confirm their alibi," I said.

Jackson did manage to avoid rolling his eyes at me and settled for a quick shake of the head.

"I'm already on it," he said. "But I'm not saying they need an alibi, got it?"

"What about the woman who was at dinner?" I said, ignoring Jackson's comment.

"Fatal Franny?" he said.

"Yeah, the supposed sharpshooter," I said.

"Apparently, she's out of town on *business*," Jackson said. "Location unknown at this point."

"Well, if anything gruesome shows up on the local news, I guess we'll know soon enough," I said, quietly.

"What's the matter, Suzy?" Jackson said. "I thought by now you'd be all jacked up and ready to go with a list of a dozen possible suspects."

I took a few minutes to explain the situation with Oslo as well as how Josie and I had spent our evening.

"The poor little guy," Jackson said. "If Sluggo had to go through something like that, I'd be a basket case."

Sluggo was Jackson's beloved bulldog and, when he wasn't on the job, his constant companion. The dog was a regular visitor at the Inn and one of our favorites.

"What did you find, Freddie?" I said, refilling the wine glasses.

"It's early," he said. "But I'm going to say it was a massive coronary."

"But before you classify it as a death by natural causes, you're going to run toxicology tests, right?" I said.

"Yes, Suzy," Freddie said, unable to resist rolling his eyes.

"Good," I said, nodding my head vigorously.

Jackson and Freddie both snorted and looked at me.

"There's no need to snort at me," I said, returning their stare. "And it's not an attractive quality."

"Why can't you just let the guy die in peace?" Jackson said. "And of all the ways a guy like Calducci could have gone out, having a heart attack on his houseboat isn't a bad option."

"It is a nice boat," Freddie said, taking a sip of wine before realizing we were both staring at him. "What? All I said was that it's a nice boat."

Chef Claire entered wearing her pajamas and running a towel through her wet hair. She draped the towel around her shoulders, poured herself a glass of wine, and slid her way onto the couch. Chloe grudgingly made room for her, then took the opportunity to stretch back out using Chef Claire's lap as a pillow.

"What did I miss?" Chef Claire said.

"I was just getting an update on Calducci's death," I said.

"Calducci? The guy who was at your table last night?" she said.

"Yeah," I said.

"He's dead?"

"You didn't know?" I said, frowning.

"How would I know? I just spent the last twelve hours feeding two hundred people," Chef Claire said.

"I assumed that Jackson or Freddie would have said something," I said.

"We came in different cars and just happened to pull into the driveway at the same time," Freddie said, beaming at Chef Claire. "Two hundred, huh? Another big night."

"Yeah, it was great. But incredibly busy," Chef Claire said, sipping her wine. "So how'd he die?"

"Heart attack," Freddie said, glancing briefly in my direction. "Most likely, natural causes."

"Maybe," I said.

"Where's Josie?" Chef Claire said.

I retold the story of how we'd spent our evening.

"So, Calducci has only been dead for a few hours, and you've already performed brain surgery on his dog?" Chef Claire said, shaking her head. "That sounds pretty weird, even for you guys."

"Well, when you say it like that, yeah," I said, laughing.

"How's the little guy doing?" Chef Claire said.

"It's too soon to tell," I said, glancing at my watch. "Josie will be heading up in a couple of hours."

"I'll get the update in the morning," Chef Claire said, yawning. "I'm beat."

"Hey, Jackson," I said. "Do you have a contact number for Mrs. Calducci? We need to give her a call about Oslo."

Jackson jotted down the number and held it in front of me just out of reach.

"Promise me you'll keep the conversation focused on the dog?" he said.

"Of course I will," I said, snatching the piece of paper from his hand. "I'm not completely insensitive to other people's feelings."

"It's not your sensitivity I'm worried about," Jackson said, laughing. "It's your snoopiness."

"I don't think that's even a word, Jackson," I said, my voice rising a notch.

"Maybe not," he said. "But you get my point, right?"

"Maybe."

I did. But I certainly wasn't about to tell him that.

Chapter 6

I dozed off sometime around five, woke just before six, and checked to make sure Oslo was comfortable. When I was sure that his vital signs were in the range Josie had outlined, I napped on and off for the next couple of hours. Josie entered the back door just after eight carrying two big mugs of coffee and headed straight for Olso's condo where I was sitting with my back against a wall and waking up for what seemed like the tenth time that morning.

"How's he doing?" she said, handing me one of the mugs.

"Thanks," I said, then took a sip before answering. "He's still stable. And he's even managed a couple of tail wags."

"That's great news. Hang in there, Oslo," she said, kneeling to gently rub the dog's leg and get a closer look at the bandage covering most of his head. Then she stood and arched her back.

"When Sammy and Jill get in I'll go over everything with them," Josie said. "And then you can head up to the house to get some sleep."

"No, I'll be fine," I said. "We need to track down Mrs. Calducci today. And I'd like to swing by Freddie's office to see what else he's figured out. We should also try to have a chat with Jackson at some point to get an update."

"Well, look who's been making a to-do list," Josie said, laughing. "You're unbelievable."

"The timing just seems suspicious," I said, climbing to my feet.

"What timing?"

"He died the night after he had dinner at our restaurant," I said. "Doesn't that bother you?"

"Not unless the man died from food poisoning," Josie said.

"Geez, I hadn't even thought of that," I said, frowning. "Now that would be a total disaster."

"Suzy, the man ate dinner every night of his life. It just so happened that his last one was at C's."

"Maybe," I said. "But you saw the looks Calducci was getting from some of the people at the restaurant. They were hostile, even hateful."

"So what?" Josie said, heading toward our reception area. "The guy was a gangster. Some people are bound to hate him."

"Maybe," I said, following her into the reception area where Sammy and Jill were behind the counter getting their morning organized.

"Suzy, would you please give it a rest?" Josie said. "It's way too early for this. Morning, guys."

"Good morning," Jill said, giving us a wide smile. Then she took a good look at us and frowned. "Gee, are you okay? You both looked exhausted."

"Hi, folks," Sammy said, glancing back and forth at us. "Yeah, I agree. Did we miss something?"

Josie gave them the short version, and they listened closely. When she finished, they both started to apologize profusely for being out of town last night.

"Stop it," Josie said, holding up a hand. "It was your night off. So don't apologize for not being at work. We were fine. And Suzy didn't faint or throw up once."

"Funny," I said, then waited out the laughter. "I'm going to go take a shower. Why don't you take Sammy and Jill through the process for Oslo, then we'll head out?"

"What makes you think I want to tag along on your wild goose chase?" Josie said, laughing.

"Well, first, because I know you're as curious as I am about what happened," I said.

"Maybe a little," Josie said, giving me a small shrug.

"Second, because I thought we'd swing by the Café for breakfast," I said. "Corned beef hash, home fries, two over-easy, sourdough toast. I'm buying."

"That's not playing fair, and you know it," she said.

"Whatever. Are you in?" I said, heading toward the back door.

"I'll be waiting in the car."

A half-hour later we made the short drive to the diner, calling Freddie and Jackson on the way to see if they'd like to join us. After I promised to pay, they both quickly agreed and were already sitting in a booth when we arrived. We sat down, greeted them, and gave our breakfast order to the waitress.

"How's the dog doing?" Jackson said.

"So far, so good," Josie said. "It'll be at least a couple more days before we'll know much more."

"What are his chances for a full recovery?" Jackson said.

"Historically, with dogs, they're pretty low," Josie said. "But I think we got it early, and if the biopsy comes back clean, his chances might be good. He's a young dog, and pretty big and strong."

"And he had the benefit of Josie's magic hands working on him," I said.

"Lucky dog," Freddie said, laughing as he glanced at Jackson.

Jackson laughed along, but they both stopped when they caught the look we were giving them.

"Really?" Josie said.

"Sorry," Freddie said. "I should know better than that by now."

"Yeah, sorry," Jackson said. "Old habits die hard."

"Forget it," Josie said. "You've got a lot of other problems on your mind."

"Yeah, like trying to walk upright," I said, laughing.

"Oh, good one," Josie said, raising her coffee mug in a mock toast.

"You know," Freddie said. "A lot of women probably would have considered that a compliment."

I glanced at Josie, then we both looked at Freddie and shook our heads.

"Shall we continue this conversation, or would you prefer to talk about something different? Maybe like how Calducci died?" I said, giving him my best crocodile smile.

"Let's go with Calducci," Freddie said.

"Yeah, let's talk about him," Jackson said. "If we stay on this topic, Freddie, you know these two will report straight back to Chef Claire."

"I know," Freddie said. "It's always three against one when it comes to Chef Claire. Neither one of us stands a chance."

"Yeah," I said, shaking my head in disbelief. "We're the reason neither one of you can make any real progress with Chef Claire." I glanced at Josie. "Do you believe these guys?"

"That's rhetorical, right?" Josie said, laughing.

"Okay, I surrender," Freddie said. "What do you want to know about Calducci?"

"Any update on the toxicology report?" I said.

"As a matter of fact, there is," Freddie said. "I stayed up all night and finished it early this morning."

"I'm impressed," I said.

"Thanks," he said. "But I didn't have much choice. I was getting a ton of pressure to get it done."

"From who?" I said.

"All the usual suspects," Freddie said, shrugging. "Our favorite FBI agent called me as soon as he heard Calducci was dead."

"You mean Chef Claire's favorite FBI agent, don't you?" Josie deadpanned.

"That's not funny, Josie. And you know it," Freddie snapped.

Agent Tompkins was an FBI agent we'd met a couple of times before. When we'd first met, he was engaged to be married, and Chef Claire, who was immediately attracted to the handsome agent, had been extremely disappointed. But the last time we'd seen Agent Tompkins, he'd informed us that the engagement was off, and Chef Claire had perked up when she heard that piece of news. And while nothing had happened between the FBI agent and Chef Claire, both Jackson and Freddie were threatened by that possibility and turned jealous every time Agent Tompkins' name came up.

"Agent Tompkins?" I said. "That's interesting."

"Not really. I find him pretty pedestrian," Freddie said.

Josie and I both snorted. Freddie ignored us and continued.

"For obvious reasons, Calducci has been on the FBI's radar for years, and they are very interested in the circumstances about how he died. And Tompkins started asking questions about the woman shooter. Had we seen her around? Did I know where she was?"

"What did you tell him?" I said, leaning forward.

"What do you think I said? I told him to do his own legwork," Freddie said.

"That probably wasn't the smartest thing to say, Freddie," Josie said.

"Hey, I don't work for the FBI," he said. "And they don't intimidate me. Especially that guy."

"That's not what I'm talking about," Josie said. "I was referring to your comment about him doing his own legwork."

"What about it?" Freddie said.

"I can't believe I have to explain it," Josie said, glancing at me.

"Yeah, I know," I said, laughing. "Slow learner."

"What are you talking about?" Freddie snapped.

"Let's say Agent Tompkins decides you're right and that he does need to do some legwork," Josie said.

"Okay," Freddie said. "I'm listening."

"And I'm so glad you called it legwork because it's really going to help drive home the point I'm about to make," Josie said, laughing.

"I can't wait to hear this," Freddie said.

"Where would Agent Tompkins have to be *physically located* to conduct this legwork?" Josie said.

Freddie sat back in the booth, then his eyes grew wide.

"I didn't think of that," he said.

"Way to go, Sherlock," Jackson said.

"I think I'll call him back later and give him a full update," Freddie said. "You know, maybe save him a trip."

"Good idea," Jackson said. "We've got enough problems with Chef Claire without him hanging around. Can you think of anything else we can tell him that might keep him away?"

"Not at the moment," Freddie said, then glanced across the table at us. "You guys have any suggestions?"

"Apart from reminding Chef Claire to shave her legs, I've got nothing," Josie deadpanned.

Josie and I laughed as we made room for our waitress who'd returned with our food. We ate in silence for a few minutes, and when it appeared that Freddie and Jackson had cooled off a bit, I restarted the conversation.

"Who else has been putting pressure on you to get the toxicology report wrapped up?" I said.

"Detective Abrams from the state police has called a couple of times," Freddie said, working his way into a big stack of pancakes. "Apparently he has a couple of open cases that have Calducci's name next to them."

"Not much gets past Detective Abrams," I said.

"No, he's really good," Josie said, dunking a piece of toast in egg yolk, then forking a pile of corned beef hash on top.

"Yeah, I like him," Freddie said, before nodding his head at Jackson. "And, of course, this guy has been calling me every half hour."

"It's not for me. I'd be happy to wait," Jackson said. "It's Howard."

"The mayor?" I said, frowning. "Why is he taking such an active interest?"

"Well, Calducci is about, what, the seventh person who's died around here since he took office?" Jackson said. "So I'm sure that's part of it. But somebody broke into Howard's place, and he's wondering if there's a connection."

I felt a jolt of adrenaline surge through me. And while the corned beef hash was excellent, I knew that it wasn't the source of my excitement.

"Somebody broke into Howard's pharmacy?" I said. "On our opening night at the restaurant?"

"Yeah, which makes sense I guess," Jackson said. "Every cop within a forty mile radius was probably there having dinner. Perfect night for a robbery."

"What did they take?" I said, starting to toy with what was left of my breakfast.

"From a pharmacy?" Jackson said, raising an eyebrow.

"Don't get snarky, Jackson," I snapped. "I meant specifically."

"It's quite a long list," Jackson said.

"You're hedging," I said, staring at Jackson.

Then a lightbulb went off, and I looked at Freddie who was doing his best to ignore me.

"You found a match, didn't you?" I said. "Calducci had a stomach full of stuff stolen from Howard's pharmacy, didn't he?"

"Maybe," Freddie said.

"Good work," Josie said, nodding at me.

"Thanks," I said, then refocused on Freddie. "What was it?"

Freddie looked at Jackson who eventually shrugged and nodded.

"Go ahead," Jackson said. "You know she won't let it go until you tell her."

"You know me so well, Jackson," I said, beaming at him. "Okay, Freddie, fess up."

"Calducci had a massive heart attack that was probably caused by a massive dose of opioids combined with a lot of alcohol," Freddie said.

"A lot?" Josie said. "Is that a technical term?"

"I could give you the total volume down to the millimeter," Freddie said. "But let's just say it was a couple of bottles of high-end spirits and leave it at that."

"What were the opioids?" I said.

"Mainly Vicodin and Percocet," Freddie said.

"Did Calducci have prescriptions for them?" I said.

"He did," Freddie said, nodding. "For chronic back pain. So it's possible it was self-inflicted."

"Suicide?" I said, shaking my head. "No, Calducci wasn't the type to do something like that."

51

"What?" Jackson said. "Mobsters can't get depressed like the rest of us?"

"I'm sure some do," I said. "But Calducci didn't seem depressed at all."

"No, not one bit," Josie said. "In fact, listening to him go on about his new dog, he sounded anything but depressed."

"Exactly," I said. "And who could be suicidal just after they got a puppy?"

"I'm not even going to try to argue with that kind of logic," Freddie said, laughing.

"You wouldn't understand," Josie said.

"Why not?" Freddie said.

"Because you're not a dog person," I said.

"What a cruel thing to say," Freddie said. "I like dogs."

"Yes, but there's a difference between someone who likes dogs and a dog person," Josie said.

"Is there now?" Freddie snapped. "Would you care to explain it?"

"A dog person would understand the difference without needing an explanation," I said.

"Exactly," Josie said, polishing off the last of her home fries.

"Unbelievable," Freddie said. "Now I'm not a dog person."

"It's not a criticism, Freddie," I said. "It's just a simple statement of fact."

"Sure. Absolutely," Jackson said. "Apart from the restaurant, that's all she's been talking about lately. I'm surprised you didn't know that."

Freddie sat quietly, then got up from the booth.

"I need to run," he said. "Thanks for breakfast. I'll see you guys around."

We watched him head out the door, then started laughing.

"That was cruel," I said.

"He deserved it," Josie said. "Where do you think he's going?"

"Probably to the Inn to check out our inventory," I said, still laughing.

"Now that I think about, maybe I should get Chef Claire-"

"It was just a joke, Jackson," Josie said, cutting him off. "Chef Claire hasn't decided to get a dog. Don't do anything stupid," Josie said.

"No, I'm serious," Jackson said. "She does love dogs as much as you two."

"She has more than enough dogs around to keep her company," Josie said. "And she's a bit busy at the moment in case you haven't noticed."

"You guys are incredibly busy and seem to manage just fine," Jackson said.

"That's because our business is dogs, Jackson," I said.

"Then why don't you do me a huge favor and just stick to doing that?" Jackson said, grinning.

I shook my head, and Josie started laughing.

"Man," I said, glancing back and forth at them. "I walked right into that one, didn't I?"

Chapter 7

After breakfast, we stopped by the restaurant after we noticed that Chef Claire's car was already parked outside. We went in the back door that led directly into the kitchen and found her standing next to the man who sold us most of the vegetables the restaurant used. Chef Claire gave us a quick wave then continued her conversation.

"Geez, I don't know, Luther," Chef Claire said, frowning. "Is that the best you can do? That's a lot of money for mizuna."

"She's buying mizuna," Josie whispered, grabbing my arm. "That means she's going to have that chicken fettuccine with the bacon-brandy cream sauce as one of the specials."

"Yum. I guess I know where we're eating dinner," I said.

A few months ago I'd never even heard of the Japanese leafy green with a peppery flavor. Now I actually preferred it to arugula, another of my favorite greens. Mizuna wasn't as bitter and did a great job soaking up broth and sauces; like the cream sauce Chef Claire used in the fettuccine dish.

"I'm sorry, Chef Claire," the man said. "We don't even grow it in our greenhouse, and it's hard to find around here."

"It can't be that hard, Luther," Chef Claire said. "The stuff will grow in your driveway."

"Yeah, but nobody else around the area uses it," he said. "Right now, you're the only one. Look, if you don't want to spend the money, why don't you substitute arugula or kale? Or maybe even the baby bok choy."

"And instead of making my chicken fettuccine with cream sauce, why don't I just order KFC?" Chef Claire said.

"Okay, okay," the man said, beaten. "I'll knock twenty percent off and talk to George about planting a couple pallets of the mizuna."

"Thank you, Luther," Chef Claire said, giving him a kiss on the cheek. "You're so good to me."

"Well, it's not like I have a choice. My wife's already warned me to make sure you stay happy," he said, laughing. "I'll see you in a couple of days."

He waved to us on his way out, and we helped Chef Claire carry the boxes of vegetables into one of the walk-in coolers. Just as we were getting ready to leave, we heard a knock on the back door. Chef Claire opened it, and a small man with bushy hair and even bushier eyebrows pushed a dolly inside and parked it next to the walk-in. He took a few seconds to catch his breath and glanced back and forth at us.

"Good morning, Morrie," Chef Claire said. "I'd like you to meet my two business partners, Suzy and Josie."

"How are you doing?" Morrie said, shaking our hands.

"Actually, we're pretty much silent partners," Josie said.

"Unless you happen to be sitting next to her while she's eating," I deadpanned.

"Funny," Josie said.

"You're the two dog people, right?" Morrie said. "You run the Doggy Inn."

"That's us," I said, smiling at him.

"How's Oslo doing?" Morrie said. "I'm pretty worried about him."

I looked at Josie, then back at Morrie. The first thing on his mind was the welfare of Calducci's dog. I decided I liked this guy. We explained what had happened and gave him an update on Oslo's condition. Morrie listened closely, then shook his head in disgust.

"I tried to warn Jimmy," Morrie said. "But he was just too smart to listen to a guy who delivers meat for a living."

"Warn him about what?" Josie said.

"About feeding Oslo all those processed meats. I mean some chicken and turkey are fine. But the nitrates in all those cold cuts can kill a dog," Morrie said.

"They wouldn't be the cause of the tumor, would they?" I said to Josie.

"Not likely," Josie said. "But they sure wouldn't help. How much did Mr. Calducci give him?"

"A lot. And all the time," Morrie said. "Every time Calducci had a sandwich or an antipasto he made sure Oslo got his share."

"Well, don't worry, Morrie," I said. "He won't be getting any more processed meats while he's with us."

"Good. What's going to happen to Oslo?" Morrie said.

"You mean, now that Calducci is dead?" I said.

"What did you think I meant?" Morrie said, giving me a hard look.

"Nothing," I whispered. "I was just asking."

"What impact will his death have on your business, Morrie?" Chef Claire said. "We've got things working great, and I'd hate to see that get screwed up."

"Don't worry, Chef Claire. Nothing will change there," Morrie said. "But I am hoping to get the thirty percent back the guy has been skimming off me for years."

"Thirty percent?" I said.

"Yeah, Jimmy was quite the guy," Morrie said. "And as you can see, I'm devastated by his death."

Morrie gave us a small smile that bordered on evil, then he relaxed and focused on the boxes he'd delivered.

"You're all set today, Chef Claire," he said. "I brought the extra forty pounds of the prime rib you asked for."

"Thanks, Morrie," Chef Claire said, glancing at Josie. "The stuff just seems to be disappearing."

"Hey, don't look at me," Josie said.

"How did you get into the meat business, Morrie?" I said.

"My wife," he said, shrugging. "She said I either had to go straight, or she was gone."

"Go straight?" I said.

"I used to be pretty well-known around the area as a second-story guy," Morrie said with a touch of pride.

"You were a burglar?" Josie said. "What did you steal?"

"Pretty much anything I could get my hands on," Morrie said, shrugging. "Then I got caught, did a year, but managed to convince my wife to stick around, and then got into business for myself."

"The meat business?" I said.

"Yeah, I bought the business from one of Calducci's cousins," he said. "I'd known Jimmy since we were kids and we, uh, *worked together* a couple of times if you know what I mean."

"Yeah, we got it," I said, laughing.

"And then Jimmy just started moving up the ranks," Morrie said. "By the time he was running the show, he'd gotten his claws into me for twenty percent off the top."

"I thought you said it was thirty," I said.

"Well, Jimmy liked to keep upping the skim every couple of years," Morrie said. "Said it helped me stay focused. Lately, he's been making noises about upping it to thirty-five. At least he was."

"I guess those days are over," I said.

"Yeah, tragic, huh?" Morrie said, beaming at me. "Okay, if you're happy, Chef Claire, I'm out of here."

"We're good, Morrie. Thanks," Chef Claire said. "It's weird, but I feel like I should be offering condolences."

"For Calducci?" Morrie said. "Save them for Oslo." Then he turned to us. "And if you get stuck finding a home for him, be sure and let me know."

"We'll do that, Morrie," Josie said. "But I need to tell you that there's no way to know how long Oslo is going to live after going through that surgery."

"So I guess he's in the same boat as the rest of us, huh?" Morrie said, shrugging.

"It's pretty hard to argue with that logic, Morrie," Josie said, laughing.

"Yeah, you might as well as save your breath when it comes to the question of how long any of us has got," he said, winking at us. "Nice meeting both of you. I'll see you soon, Chef Claire."

We watched him until his truck rumbled away, then Chef Claire closed the door. She motioned for us to follow her to the far end of the kitchen. Josie and I glanced at the table with six chairs tucked away in the corner.

"Is that what I think it is?" Josie said.

"It is," Chef Claire said. "I didn't really want to do it, but your mom just kept harping on about how we needed a chef's table in the kitchen."

"It looks great," Josie said, glancing around. "And it's out of the way so it shouldn't bother you or your staff, right?"

"No, it's fine," Chef Claire said. "But I'll have to watch my language."

Normally sweet and kind, we'd learned during the time she'd been living with us that Chef Claire had a tendency to swear like a sailor when things got crazy in the kitchen.

"Have you started taking reservations yet?" Josie said.

"Yeah, Mrs. C. has put permanent dibs on Wednesday nights all summer, but I'm sure we can squeeze you in," Chef Claire said, laughing. "But I'd prefer it if you'd fill all six seats. I'm going to be doing a seven-course tasting menu, and six is the perfect number for what I'm making."

"Oh, we'll fill the table," I said.

"Or make sure we eat all the leftovers," Josie said.

"Now there's a shock," Chef Claire said. "Who do you have in mind inviting?"

"Oh, probably just the usual suspects," Josie said, grinning at me. "You know, Sammy and Jill, Jackson, Freddie…maybe Agent Tompkins if he's in the area."

"Agent Tompkins, huh?" Chef Claire said, cocking her head. "Interesting. At the same table with Jackson and Freddie?"

"Sure," I said.

"Do you really think that's a good idea?" Chef Claire said.

"We think it's a great idea, Chef Claire," Josie said, laughing.

"I have to admit that I'd love to see him," Chef Claire said. "But I don't want to upset Jackson and Freddie. I love both of them." She exhaled loudly and seemed to be fighting back the tears.

I glanced at Josie who nodded for me to proceed. It was a question we'd been dying to ask her but hadn't been able to summon up the courage.

"Yes, we know. And we feel the same way," I said. "But you're not *in love* with either one of them, are you?"

"No," she said with a sad shake of her head. "At least, not yet."

"Well, I guess there's no real hurry for you to make up your mind," Josie said. "It's not like you're going anywhere."

"No, I'm never leaving this place," she said. "And that's why I need to be very careful about the decisions I make. And how I handle Jackson and Freddie."

She seemed wound tighter than a ball of string, and I felt bad about bringing it up in the first place. She wiped her eyes with the back of her sleeve and loudly exhaled again.

"I've been thinking that maybe I *should* get a puppy," she said, laughing. "It always seems to work for the two of you."

"You'll never go wrong with a puppy," I said. "And we'd be happy to keep an eye on it whenever you're busy."

"I have no doubt about that," she said, finally managing a smile.

"What kind of dog would you get?" Josie said.

"I've always wanted a Golden Retriever," she said.

"Great call. And I think a Golden would fit in great with Captain and Chloe," I said.

"You guys never worry about having too many dogs around, do you?" Chef Claire said.

"Too many dogs is impossible, Chef Claire. You should know that by now," I said, laughing.

64

"Yeah, I guess I should," she said. "So, you wouldn't have a problem with it?"

"Not at all," I said, glancing at Josie.

"I think it's a great idea," Josie deadpanned. "Suzy and I collect dogs the same way you seem to attract male admirers."

"That's not funny, Josie," Chef Claire said, gently punching her on the arm.

"Disagree."

Chapter 8

We finally managed to track down the widow Calducci early the next day. And since we'd caught her early in the morning, she sounded intelligent and coherent over the phone. But she spoke in a muted tone Josie and I attributed to the shock of losing her husband. After we explained Oslo's situation, she reluctantly agreed to swing by the Inn around lunchtime.

Josie had decided to keep Oslo mildly sedated after he'd woken from surgery and had immediately started trying to scratch the stitches in his head. Post-surgery sedation wasn't the norm, and Josie hated doing it, but she'd been left with no choice since the dog, with one well-placed scratch, could do himself some real damage and undo several hours of her intricate work. He was resting comfortably but continued to run a fever Josie was starting to get concerned about. But he did greet everyone who stopped by his condo with a few thumps of his tail. Given all the challenges Olso was dealing with, I considered that a good sign.

At eleven thirty, Dot Calducci and Pee Wee walked through the front door and glanced around the reception area. Josie and I were standing behind the check-in counter talking with Sammy and Jill and glanced up when we heard them come in. Dot and Pee Wee were wearing matching sunglasses and looked like they were dressed for golf.

Pee Wee's bald head gleamed from the overhead fluorescent lights, and he looked even bigger than I remembered from opening night. Doubting that the size of his head and massive torso had come naturally, I found myself wondering if he went through steroids the same way Josie went through a bag of the bite-sized Snickers. As I studied him, I decided that if I had to choose somebody to keep Calducci quiet and immobilized while someone else stuffed handfuls of opioids down his throat, Pee Wee would probably be number one on my list.

I was intrigued by that idea but realized I was getting way ahead of myself. This conversation was supposed to focus on Oslo, and the question of who might have killed Calducci would have to wait.

"Good morning," I said, smiling at them as the caboose of my train of thought finally left the station.

"Yes, good morning," Dot said, removing her sunglasses. "Okay, I'm here."

Her eyes were red and puffy, and I decided that she had either just finished a good cry, or had a hangover that would kill a horse. Maybe both.

"We were very sorry to hear about your husband, Mrs. Calducci," I said.

"Yes, we certainly are," Josie said. "Please accept our deepest condolences."

"Thank you," she whispered.

It was probably the hundredth time she'd had this conversation the past few days, and I felt sorry for her. Wherever her marriage had ended up, at one point, she must have been a very happy woman. And I hoped as time passed the good memories would drown out the more recent that were, based on everything we'd heard, a collection of hazy, alcohol-soaked days that blurred together.

"You said over the phone that you wanted to talk about my husband's dog," the widow Calducci said, obviously anxious to get started.

"Of course," I said, gesturing for them to follow us. "Oslo's resting in his condo."

"Condo?" she said.

"Yes," I said, leading the way.

"Wouldn't the term cage be more accurate?" she said.

"No, it wouldn't," Josie said, forcing a smile as she glanced over her shoulder.

I smiled to myself. The widow Calducci might be grieving, and we would do everything we could to support her. But she needed to be careful about her choice of words today when it came to dogs. Josie was still steamed about Dot calling Oslo an idiot at dinner and, bad puns aside, was on a very short leash.

We stopped in front of Oslo's condo, and he looked up and thumped his tail a few times before lowering his head down on top of his front paws.

"Would you like to go inside and pet him?" I said to Dot.

68

"No, that's quite alright," she said, staring at the bandages wrapped around the dog's head. "You mentioned brain surgery. Is it going to be okay?"

"We're still not sure," Josie said. "But we're hoping *he* makes a full recovery."

If Dot caught the intent of Josie's response, she did a good job ignoring it.

"So we were wondering what you'd like to do about Oslo," I said.

"What do you mean what I'd like to do?" Dot said, frowning as she glanced at Pee Wee.

"Well, since Oslo was your husband's dog, it would stand to reason that custody would transfer to you," I said.

"That makes sense," Pee Wee said, nodding.

"Does it now?" Dot said, glaring at Pee Wee before looking back at me. "Yes, it was my husband's dog. And since it was, it has nothing to do with me."

"I see," I whispered.

"This is a total waste of my time," the widow snapped. "I suppose you dragged me out here just so you could give me the bill in person, right?"

My ability to support her during her grieving period was rapidly dwindling, and I noticed Josie's eyes had turned dark.

"We're only interested in Oslo's well-being, Mrs. Calducci," Josie whispered.

"His well-being? Really? Condos? Custody?" she said, bewildered. "I can't believe I'm having this conversation. Is this really the sort of thing you spent your life doing?"

"Yeah, pretty much," Josie said, shrugging and glancing at me for confirmation.

"It's a living," I said, forcing what would probably be my last fake smile.

"What on earth is wrong with you two?" the widow Calducci said, laughing.

"Actually, there are a lot of theories floating around about that question," I said. "So, I take it that you aren't interested in taking Oslo after he recovers."

"Finally," she said, shaking her head. "You've said something that actually makes sense. No, of course, I don't want the stupid dog."

I noticed Josie clenching and unclenching her fists and placed a hand on her arm.

"That's fine, Mrs. Calducci," I said. "All you need to do is sign a form transferring ownership to us, and you can leave anytime you like."

"Where do I sign?" she said.

"Just head back out to the reception area. Sammy has the form ready," I said.

She wheeled and walked away. Pee Wee watched her go then moved closer to Oslo's condo.

"You really did brain surgery on him?" Pee Wee said.

"Yeah," Josie said, still trying to calm herself down.

"That's amazing," he said, staring at Oslo who was napping on his thick dog bed. "How long did you have to go to school to learn how to do that?"

"A very long time," Josie said. "Including undergrad, vet school, and my residency, it was about a decade."

"Wow," Pee Wee said. "You must have really wanted to be a vet."

"More than anything."

"You think he's going to be okay?"

"We hope so," Josie said, staring into the condo.

"Did you spend much time with Oslo?" I said.

"Nah," Pee Wee said, shaking his head. "Mr. Calducci went everywhere with him, and since Jimmy and Dot did everything they could to avoid being in the same room at the same time, I didn't see that much of the dog."

"That's because you work for her, don't you?" I said.

"Well done. You're pretty smart," Pee Wee said.

"I have my moments."

"Most people always assumed I worked for him, but she was the one who hired me a couple of years ago."

"To be her bodyguard?" I said, leaning against the wall.

Since it appeared he was in the mood to chat, I decided to do my best to come across as casual.

"Yeah, that's how it started," Pee Wee said. "The job has changed a bit since then."

I passed on the chance to steer the conversation toward the nature of their personal relationship. Josie's observations at dinner had provided me all the details I needed to hear about that. But the rationale behind his initial hiring intrigued me.

"Why would Mrs. Calducci need a bodyguard?" I said.

"Look, I probably shouldn't even be having this conversation, but I'm running out of options. Maybe you two might have some ideas. Dot, uh, tends to get paranoid at times," he said quietly. "Especially at night."

"And it's not because she's afraid of the dark, right?" I said.

"No," he said, chuckling. "Dot kinda likes it dark."

"She turns paranoid when she drinks?" I said.

"Yeah, among other things," Pee Wee said, giving us a sad smile. "It's bad, and it's getting worse."

"But who would she need protection from?" Josie said.

"She has a long list of possibilities," he said. "Most of them are people associated with Mr. Calducci's operation, but it's all in her imagination. They wouldn't go after her. Primarily, she was paranoid about him."

"Her husband?" I said, glancing at Josie.

"Yeah," Pee Wee said. "She and Jimmy had some knockdown, drag-out battles that were legendary. There were a couple of fights even I didn't want to get in the middle of. Can you believe that?"

"Based on your size, no," Josie said, smiling at him.

"Did they get violent with each other?" I said.

"Well, you and I probably have a different definition of what constitutes violence," he said, for some reason finding his comment funny. "But, yeah. From time to time they were known to smack each other around."

"Interesting," I said.

I didn't have a clue why I said it out loud.

"Not really," Pee Wee said. "Just a crappy marriage. Look, I need to get going. It's almost time for lunch, and I need to make sure I get some food in her stomach before she starts hitting the Bloody Marys."

"Okay. Thanks for bringing her by," I said.

"No problem," he said. "And take good care of that little guy. I hate to see him like that."

"We'll do everything we can, Pee Wee," Josie said.

He started to head back to the reception area, then stopped and turned around.

"So you did all those tests and the operation even though you knew you probably wouldn't get paid for it?" he said.

"Yeah," Josie said.

"Hmmm," he said, giving the matter serious thought. "How much would the bill be?"

"Probably somewhere around fifteen thousand," Josie said.

"Wow," he said. "But after watching how much happier Mr. Calducci was after he got the dog, I can see why people would fork that much out if they had it."

He waved and headed off to the reception area. We watched him leave, then looked at each other.

"What do you know?" Josie said. "Pee Wee's a dog person."

"Yeah, who would have thought?" I said.

"Are they still on the list of suspects?" Josie said.

"Oh, yeah," I said. "As soon as he described their fights, Dot went right to the top of the list."

"What about Pee Wee?" Josie said.

"I'm not sure about him," I said. "But whoever managed to get all those pills in Calducci would probably have needed some help, right?"

"Unless Calducci was already passed out," Josie said. "Freddie said he had a ton of booze in his system."

"But why kill him now?" I said, taking a look around the condo area to make sure all the dogs were settled in comfortably.

"Maybe it was the cumulative effect," Josie said. "All those years of bad history certainly must have taken their toll."

"Yeah, and maybe the opportunity just presented itself," I said.

"I can definitely see the widow as a suspect," Josie said.

"Yeah, maybe," I said, already second-guessing myself.

Josie snorted.

"Unbelievable," she said. "One minute ago, she was on the top of your list."

"I know," I said. "But it's way too early. We haven't even talked with any of Calducci's business associates. Not to mention tracking down Fatal Franny."

"I hate to argue with you, Suzy, but wouldn't have Fatal Franny just shot him?"

"Maybe," I said. "But Calducci overdosing on booze and pills would certainly keep the focus off her, right?"

"Yeah, it probably would," she conceded.

"And let's not forget Morrie the Meat Guy," I said.

"Oh, let's not drag him into this," Josie said. "He seems like such a sweet old man."

"A sweet old man with a criminal history and years of Calducci taking advantage of him," I said, raising an eyebrow.

"So, you're saying we've got more work to do?" Josie said, laughing.

"Oh, yeah," I said, nodding.

"Suzy, if this turns out to be nothing more than an accident or suicide, I'm going to get very cranky," Josie said.

"Thanks for the warning. But it's not a suicide," I said.

I stared at the far wall deep in thought. I was brought back by the familiar mouse-like crinkle of foil being unwrapped.

"You want a bite-sized?" Josie said, extending the bag toward me.

"Maybe just a small handful, thanks."

Chapter 9

Even though Jimmy Calducci had left Clay Bay at an early age, he had decided at some point in life to be buried in the town where he'd been born. As such, Josie and I found ourselves standing outside St. Benedictine's waiting for my mother to find the perfect parking spot. It needed to be a shady spot and one that would provide other people with the chance to notice her arrival and marvel at how good she looked. But it couldn't be too far away where she'd be forced to work up a sweat on her stroll toward the church.

Not that my mother would ever admit to being that calculating. It was just one of those personality quirks that became intuitive to a daughter as time passed.

But I had to admit that she looked fantastic.

And stayed dry.

"Hello, darling," she said, bussing my cheek. "Thanks for coming. I don't think I could have gotten through this all by myself." She hugged and kissed Josie. "Hello, dear."

"Hi, Mrs. C.," Josie said. "Sorry to hear about Mr. Calducci."

"Yes, it's tragic," she said, blinking back tears. "Despite all his considerable flaws, Jimmy was a good man."

Out of respect for the deceased, I kept my opinions about the dead gangster to myself and nodded.

"Sure, sure," I said, then gestured toward the front door of the church. "Shall we go inside?"

My mother nodded, and Josie and I each took one of her arms on the way up the steps. I waited for my mother to step through the open doors then paused at the entrance.

"Worried about bursting into flames?" Josie whispered.

"Maybe a little. It's been a while since I've been here," I whispered, as I moved to one side to let other people walk past me.

"Tell me about it," Josie whispered. "My mother would kill me if she knew how long it's been since I've been to Mass."

"Do you think any of the rules have changed?" I whispered.

"I don't think so," Josie said, frowning. "But who knows? Look, if we just stick to the basics, we should be fine."

"I'm going to need a little clarification," I said, waving to a couple of friends on their way inside.

"Pay close attention during the stand, sit, kneel parts of the service, and don't chug the wine," Josie said.

I stifled a laugh and followed her to a pew my mother had commanded near the back of the church. Nervous, and feeling completely out of my element, I patted my mother's knee in a show of comfort and took a look around. Dozens of people I didn't know were scattered throughout the church, and I assumed they were business associates of Calducci from out of town. At the far end of a pew near the back of the church, I noticed Morrie the Meat Guy sitting quietly by himself. In the front row, I saw

Dot and Pee Wee sitting next to each other in an otherwise empty pew. Dot had her sunglasses on, and Pee Wee was wearing a tailored suit that must have been fitted before his more recent rounds of steroids and gym work.

"Is it my imagination, or does Pee Wee look even bigger today?" I said, nudging Josie.

"Yeah, he's a bruiser," Josie said. "You know, one time when I was in vet school, I had a date with a guy who had muscles like that."

"You're joking, right?" I said, glancing at her.

"It was a blind date," she whispered, then frowned as she searched her memory bank. "I think he played lacrosse. Or one of those other sports you get to hit people with a stick."

"How was it?"

"About what you might expect," Josie said. "Once we got past hello, we pretty much ran out of things to talk about."

"Your basic; nice house, nobody home?" I said, laughing loud enough to get a glare out of my mother.

"Exactly," Josie said, laughing.

"Ladies, please. Show some respect for the dead," my mother whispered through clenched teeth.

"Sorry, Mom," I said. "Should I add that one to my list of sins I need to confess?"

"You don't need to worry about going to confession, darling."

"Really? Why not?"

"Because I really don't want to sit here all day and have to wait for you," my mother said, giving me a small smile.

"Funny," I said.

"Sorry, I'm late, folks."

We glanced up at the mayor who was sliding into our pew. He worked his way past Josie and me, then sat down on the other side of my mother.

"Hello, Howard," my mother said, giving him a crocodile smile. "It's so nice to see our mayor finally make an appearance."

"Did I miss anything?" he said, ignoring my mother's crack and nodding hello at us.

"No. But I thought you were coming to the viewing last night," my mother said.

"I got tied up at the pharmacy, then I had a few things to take care of down at town hall," Howard said, glancing around the church. "Good crowd. But I bet most of them are here just to make sure he's really dead."

I chuckled under my breath. But it still garnered another glare from my mother.

"Howard," my mother said, elbowing him. "Stop that. Show some respect."

"Sorry," Howard said, grinning at me.

"Any luck finding out who might have robbed your place, Howard?" I whispered.

"No," he said, shaking his head. "Jackson said that whoever did it knew what they were doing. No prints of any kind. They pretty much cleaned out my drug supplies."

"That really sucks, Howard," I said. "Sorry to hear that."

"Shhh," my mother said, squeezing my knee.

"Ow," I whispered, as I squirmed away from her vice-like grip. "Geez, Mom. That hurt."

"It's supposed to hurt," my mother said as she casually glanced around the church.

Pee Wee could learn a few things from my mother about inflicting pain.

A priest I didn't recognize began the service, and I tried to follow the crowd as they effortlessly followed the ritual. I felt like a teenager at a school dance who was trying to fake her way through the latest dance craze, and at one point I found myself kneeling while the rest of the congregation was already sitting back in their seats. Embarrassed, I eased myself back into a sitting position trying to appear casual while doing it.

Josie stifled a snort, and I glared at her.

"Smooth," she whispered.

"Shut up," I said.

"Good advice," my mother said, glaring at me. "Take it."

After the mass, several people offered testimonials to the man known as Jimmy Calducci. Most were reverent, some were funny, while others included details about the dead man that were completely lost on me. The air conditioning wasn't doing its job, and I found myself starting to nod off a few times. Fortunately, my mother was sitting next to me, and her sharp elbow kept me awake, if not entirely alert.

Calducci's widow gave a short tribute to her husband and thanked everyone for coming. When she finished, I assumed that the service was over and started thinking about lunch. I was halfway out of my seat when Josie nudged me, and I sat back down and followed her eyes. A woman slowly approached the altar, and the priest stared at her. Initially, he took a few steps back to give her room as she got closer. Then it appeared he wanted to get as far away as he could and walked to the far end of the altar and sat down staring off into the distance.

"Think the priest might be worried about getting caught in the crossfire?" Josie whispered.

"Yeah, if he could get away with it, he'd be sitting in the vestibule," I whispered.

"Will you two please stop?" my mother said, but unable to stifle a giggle.

I watched as Fatal Franny, wearing a short black skirt with matching jacket, faced the crowd. If it weren't for the slight bulge I noticed under her jacket, she could have easily passed for a corporate executive.

"She's packing in church?" I whispered.

"Maybe she was having trouble accessorizing all that black," Josie whispered.

Fatal Franny tugged her lapels back into place, stood behind the podium, and gripped it tightly with both hands. She gave the entire congregation a menacing glare before she started speaking without notes.

"I know that Jimmy would have appreciated all of you for coming today to show your respect," Fatal Franny said in a flat, clipped tone. "I also want to thank all of you for being here. And I especially want to thank one very special individual. And that's the person who did this to Jimmy. Because I know you're here, and I have something very specific I want to say. And I want to make sure you hear it directly from me just so we're clear."

I didn't think it was possible for a silent room to get even quieter, but it did. And Fatal Franny let the silence throughout the church hang like a shroud over the entire congregation before continuing.

"Jimmy was a great man," she said, quietly. "A great man. And none of you will ever know all of the things he did for other people in his life. None of you will ever know him like I did."

Fatal Franny fixed a glare directly on Calducci's widow in the front row and held it for several seconds. I couldn't see the expression on Dot's face, but I was pretty sure it must have been a blend of fear and a deep concern about bladder control. Fatal Franny eventually refocused her stare on the congregation and, like everyone else in the church, I was convinced she was looking directly at me.

"That is one scary woman," I whispered.

"Yeah," Howard said, leaning closer to me. "But there's something about her that's really appealing."

"Howard, please don't tell me you've got the hots for that hit woman," my mother whispered.

"No, it's not that," he whispered. "Well, maybe it is. She's a good looking woman."

"Unbelievable," my mother said.

Josie leaned over in front of me and looked at Howard.

"Just remember one thing, Howard," Josie said.

"What's that?"

"Don't cheat on her," Josie deadpanned.

My mother and I laughed along with several people sitting close enough to hear our exchange. Fatal Franny heard the noise and glared in our direction. We settled back into our seats, red-faced.

"I want to speak directly to the person who took Jimmy from us. And, yes, I am certain that you are here with all of us today. Perhaps you're here because, if you weren't, it would look suspicious. Or you're here because of some weird need for closure. Or maybe you needed to witness firsthand the results of your work."

Fatal Franny paused one more time for effect and glanced around the church with her perfected menacing glare.

"Whatever the reason, you can rest assured about one simple fact. I am going to hunt you down. And I am going to make you pay for what you've done."

Then Fatal Franny left the podium, walked down the steps, then slowly made her way down the center aisle, her footsteps echoing the entire way until she departed through the front door. The priest offered another thank you and a quick final prayer, then disappeared through a door at the back of the altar.

"Wow," Josie said, standing up. "A funeral and a death threat. That's a first."

"You don't think she was just trying to deflect attention from herself as a possible suspect, do you?" I said.

"I guess anything's possible," Josie said, shrugging. "But in the interest of personal safety, I'm going to take her at her word."

"Yeah," I said, nodding. "Good call. After all that, I think lunch at C's is called for."

"I could eat."

"How about you guys?" I said to Howard and my mother. "You feel like joining us? I'm buying."

"How could I refuse an offer to have lunch with three beautiful women?" Howard said, giving us a slight bow.

"That's great, Howard," Josie deadpanned. "But don't get your hopes up. None of us are packing today."

"I'm glad to hear that, Josie," the mayor said, grinning.

"But be careful, Howard," I said, heading for the front door. "She's lethal with a knife and fork."

Chapter 10

The restaurant was busy, and several people were taking advantage of the warm weather to sit outside on the wraparound verandah. Many had brought their dogs, and most of them were sipping cocktails and studying both the regular menu and the dog version we'd helped Chef Claire put together. My mother and Howard headed inside while Josie and I stopped to chat with several friends and their dogs. After we'd exchanged pleasantries and finally managed to tear ourselves away from a pair of Lab puppies that were the life of the party, we headed for the kitchen. We said a quick hello to Chef Claire, who paused long enough to look up from the long line of order slips to flash a smile and wave, then she shooed us out of the kitchen. We joined my mother and the mayor at her table.

"Poor Jimmy. I'm going to miss him," my mother said, not glancing up from her menu. "But that was a nice service."

"I thought it was bizarre," I said, not bothering to open my menu.

"Yes, perhaps," my mother said, still not looking up. "But it seemed appropriate given the way Jimmy lived his life."

"I agree with Suzy," Howard said, taking a sip of water. "It was weird."

"Speaking of weird," I said, watching as the woman approached our table. "Look sharp, Howard."

85

"What?" Howard said, turning in his seat. "Oh, hi. It's nice to see you."

Fatal Franny stopped a few feet away from our table and nodded at Howard, then gave the rest of us a small smile.

"Hi, Franny," I said. "That was quite the testimonial you gave at the service."

"Thanks," she said. "I was nervous. I've never done anything like that before."

"You mean like scare a large group of people half to death?" Josie said, smiling up at her.

"Oh, you thought I came across as scary?" Fatal Franny said.

"Actually, Franny, to be honest, I thought you were terrifying," Josie said.

"Good," Fatal Franny said, nodding. "That's what I was going for."

"Would you like to join us for lunch?" my mother said, setting her menu down.

Fatal Franny considered the invitation, then nodded and sat down next to me.

"I would. That's very kind of you," Franny said, unfolding her napkin and draping it across her lap. "And thanks again for dinner the other night. It was a wonderful evening."

I glanced at Josie who gave me a small shrug. For a hit woman, Fatal Franny seemed to be a bit of an enigma. One minute she was threatening to rip somebody's spleen out, the next she was a composed professional woman demurely perusing the wine list.

"What do you recommend?" Fatal Franny said.

"The Josie," the rest of us at the table said simultaneously.

"When did you have my sandwich?" Josie said, looking across the table at Howard.

"I was here for lunch yesterday," he said. "Chef Claire recommended it. It's incredible."

"You have a sandwich named after you?" Fatal Franny said. "I'm impressed."

"Thanks," Josie said, puffed with pride.

"What's in it?"

"Well, Chef Claire takes a waffle fluffy enough to double as a pillow and cuts it in half horizontally," Josie said, her eyes dancing. "Then she slathers both sides with this homemade apple butter that'll bring tears to your eyes. Next come layers of lettuce and tomato, followed by four thick slices of bacon. Then she puts an over easy egg on top and covers it with the other half of the waffle."

"It sounds great," Fatal Franny said, nodding.

"It's a total knee-buckler," I said.

Our waitress approached carrying a pitcher of iced tea. She poured then asked for our orders.

"It sounds like everyone is going to have The Josie, Amanda," my mother said, glancing around the table to make sure she was right.

"Good choice," the waitress said, beaming at Josie. "Will that be all?"

"You're joking, right, Amanda?" Josie said.

"Of course, I'm joking," she said, laughing. "What else can I bring you?"

"I'll have an order of fries," Josie said, concentrating hard. "And a couple orders of the stuffed mushrooms for the table. Oh, and one of the small antipasto."

"Yeah, let's stick with the small one," I said. "You wouldn't want people to think you were a little piggy."

"I'm pretty sure people already know I'm a little piggy," Josie said, organizing her cutlery.

The waitress chuckled and headed for the kitchen. Josie noticed Fatal Franny staring at her with a puzzled expression.

"Funerals always make me hungry," Josie said, shrugging.

"So, Franny," Howard said. "Based on what you said at the service, am I correct assuming that you'll be in town awhile?"

"Yeah, I'll be around from time to time," she said, adjusting the bulge under her jacket. "Why do you want to know?"

"Oh, I just thought you might be interested in a little tour of the River," Howard said. "You know, pack a lunch, take my boat out, and enjoy the sunshine."

Fatal Franny considered the mayor's invitation for several moments then nodded.

"Sure. That sounds good," she said, giving Howard a smile.

"That's great," he said. "How about tomorrow?"

"If we can do it in the afternoon," she said. "I have something I need to take care of in the morning."

Then her eyes drifted off to another table on the other side of the restaurant and stayed there. I snuck a glance at the table and recognized the four men from Calducci's service. Fatal Franny continued to stare at them, then stood up.

"If you'll excuse me for a moment," Fatal Franny said. "I need to have a quick word with the gentlemen at that table."

We watched her depart just as the waitress arrived with the stuffed mushrooms and antipasto. We started nibbling, and Josie and I took full advantage of our vantage point to keep an eye on Fatal Franny's interaction with the other table.

"What's going on over there?" my mother whispered.

"Well, it's a quiet conversation, but I'd have to say it's anything but casual," I said.

"Yeah," Josie said, selecting several items from the antipasto and filling a small plate. "Judging by the look on that one guy's face, she seems to be warning them about something."

"She wouldn't have to warn me twice," I said, popping a mushroom into my mouth. "I can't believe you asked her out, Howard."

"Why not?" Howard said. "We're both single adults."

"A nice little tour of the islands, followed by an extended stop at Lover's Cove?" I said.

"More like a layover, right, Howard?" Josie said, laughing. "I wonder if she leaves her holster on."

"Don't be disgusting, Josie," my mother said, giving her the evil eye. "We're trying to eat here."

"Sorry, Mrs. C.," Josie said.

"As always, I'm going to be the perfect gentleman," the mayor said, turning smarmy. "We'll take a pleasant little cruise, followed by a picnic lunch, and perhaps a nice bottle of wine. Of course, if she were so inclined, I'd be-"

"Shut it, Howard," my mother said.

"Yeah," Josie said, laughing. "We're trying to eat here."

Chapter 11

We headed back to the Inn after lunch to check in with Sammy and Jill and see how Oslo was doing. He managed to stand when he saw us enter the condo area and wagged his tail. Then he tentatively walked across the condo until he reached the door and sat down. I opened the door, and Josie and I stepped inside and closed the door behind us. We both sat down and gently stroked the dog's fur. Josie gave the bandage covering most of his head a quick examination and decided it was good to go for another day.

"He wasn't listing when he walked across the condo," I said. "That's good news, right?"

"That's very good news," Josie said, moving her finger back and forth in front of Oslo's eyes and studying his reaction. "Good boy."

"He seems a lot more alert," I said.

"He definitely is," Josie said. "But don't get your hopes up, Suzy. He's got a long way to go."

"I know he's going to make it," I said, firmly.

"He better," Josie said, laughing. "If he doesn't, you'll never forgive me."

"No, I would," I said. "Eventually."

We headed to my office and spent an hour dealing with some Inn business, including our most recent financial statements.

"How about that?" I said. "We actually made a little money last month. I don't think we've ever turned a profit in April before."

"Wonders never cease," Josie said. "And May should be a good month. I think our reputation is growing."

"As it should," I said, accepting the bag of bite-sized from her.

We looked up when we heard the knock on the door.

"Come in," I said.

The head of the crew handling our expansion project entered and gave us a small wave and a smile.

"You guys got a minute?" he said.

"Sure, Justin," I said. "Have a seat. What's up?"

"I just wanted to let you know that we just finished putting up all the drywall today," he said, selecting a bite-sized from the bag Josie was extending toward him. "Thanks."

"You're done already?" I said, glancing at the calendar on my computer screen. "Three days ahead of schedule?"

"Yeah," he said, nodding. "This new guy I just brought on is incredible. When it comes to drywall, this guy is a rock star."

"That's great," I said. "So you're ready to start painting and doing the finishing work?"

"Yeah, we're going to get started tomorrow."

"Amazing," Josie said, over the sound of the mouse-like crinkle.

"We've been thinking about doing a bit of work up at the house," I said. "Does this new guy handle electrical and plumbing?"

"This guy does everything," he said. "If you like, I'll bring him by tomorrow and introduce him."

"Good," I said. "Where did you find this guy anyway?"

"He just showed up the other day looking for a job. He says he used to work for that dead gangster. You know, Jimmy Calducci."

I looked at Josie who seemed as surprised and confused as I was.

"Yeah, please bring him by," I said. "We'd love to meet him."

"You got it," he said, accepting one more of the bite-sized before standing. "Thanks. I'll see you guys tomorrow. Oh, if it's all right with you, I'd like to knock off early today and take the crew down to the Water's Edge for a bit of a celebration. They've been busting their hump on this job."

"Absolutely," I said, nodding. "And just tell Millie to put it on my tab. Food and drinks are on me."

"Gee, thanks, Suzy," he said, glancing back and forth at us. "You guys are the best."

"We have our moments," I said.

When he'd departed, I leaned back in my chair.

"That's interesting," I said. "You think it's a coincidence that the guy showed up right after Calducci died?"

"I'm gonna go fifty-fifty on that question until I know a bit more," Josie said. "But if somebody wanted to find out who might have killed Calducci, I guess a construction guy would make a pretty good spy."

"Yes, he would," I said. "Hang around the bars, get in good with some of the locals, and do some quiet snooping over a few beers. But who would have sent him here?"

"It could be anybody on our suspect list," Josie said. "Or somebody we haven't crossed paths with yet."

"Yeah, that's a good point. Instead of being the killer, any of our suspects might actually be trying to figure out who killed Calducci."

"That could make things a bit tricky, huh?" Josie said, crumpling the empty bag of Snickers.

"Yeah," I said, my mind racing in several directions. "So, we've got Dot, Pee Wee, Fatal Franny, and Morrie the Meat Guy."

"I really can't see Morrie involved," Josie said. "He's such a sweet guy."

"And Calducci was a dog person," I said, raising an eyebrow at her. "What's your point?"

"Yeah, I know," she said. "But I hope it's not Morrie."

"Me too," I said. "And given the way Fatal Franny's conversation at lunch seemed to go, I guess we should add the four guys from that table to our list."

"Why not?" Josie said, laughing. "The more, the merrier. Maybe we should just get a copy of the guest book from the funeral service. We wouldn't want to miss anybody."

"You're not funny," I said.

"Disagree."

"And we should probably add the construction guy, too."

"Geez, Suzy," Josie said, shaking her head. "Can we at least meet the guy before you suspect him of being a murderer?"

"I guess you've got a good point there," I said, making room for Chloe as she jumped up in my lap. I rubbed her head and left my arm draped over her after she got herself situated. "I've been thinking about something else. Why do you think Fatal Franny agreed to go out on the boat with Howard?"

"Maybe it's just a simple question of mutual attraction," Josie said.

"Maybe," I said.

"Or she's looking for some information about who might have broken into Howard's pharmacy," Josie said.

"There you go," I said, nodding. "I was thinking the exact same thing."

"And she's got a couple ways to get it out of him, right?" she said, grinning.

"Oh, I doubt if she'll have to use her gun to get Howard talking," I said, laughing.

"Yeah, that's highly unlikely," Josie said. "But in her job, it's probably nice to have that option to fall back on."

"You know, if I remember, we were talking about taking the dogs out on the boat tomorrow," I said.

"And you think that we should keep an eye out for Howard and Fatal Franny?" Josie said. "Maybe swing by to say hello."

"Well, it couldn't hurt," I said.

"Unbelievable," she said, pulling a fresh bag of the bite-sized from her purse. "Okay but if we swing by Lover's Cove at some point and see Howard's boat there, we're going to approach with caution. If it even appears that they're getting busy, we're out of there immediately. I like Howard, but there is no way I want to see that."

"Yuk," I said, frowning. "You'll get no argument from me."

"Good. So what do you want to do for dinner?" Josie said.

"Well, we were just there for lunch, but I guess we could swing by the restaurant," I said.

"Yeah, after all, it's about the only chance we get to see Chef Claire these days," Josie said.

"Absolutely," I said, nodding. "I miss her."

Josie snorted.

"What?" I said.

"We're rationalizing," she said.

"Totally."

"The restaurant has completely spoiled us."

"Without a doubt," I said.

"You feel bad about it?"

"Not yet," I said, shaking my head.

"Yeah, me neither."

Chapter 12

As promised, Justin brought the new member of his work crew by my office first thing the next morning. The man's name was Rocco, and he was middle-aged but ripped from the waist up. Judging from the scar tissue around his nose and eyes, it looked like he might have boxed earlier in his life. Either that or he was an aficionado of bar fights. But he seemed friendly enough, and he immediately gave Captain and Chloe a lot of attention and affection when he met them.

"How's Oslo doing?" Rocco said, looking up from the vigorous head scratch he was giving Captain.

"He's doing pretty well," Josie said. "Considering everything he's been through."

"I tried to tell Jimmy something was wrong with him," Rocco said. "But he was convinced the dog was just a little goofy." He glanced at Josie. "But you only needed to take one look at him before you knew he had a problem?"

"Yeah, pretty much," Josie said. "It wasn't hard to spot."

"I tried to tell him," Rocco said, shaking his head as he started wrestling with Captain on the floor. "This guy is great."

We let the scene play out, and then Rocco followed the dogs and us up the path that led to the house. We showed him the small bathroom off the living room we'd be thinking about remodeling for a while. Josie explained what we wanted to do, and he listened closely, asked for clarification a few times, and then nodded.

"Okay, that's all I need," he said. "If you've got some paper, I'll work up a quote right now."

"Let's go to the kitchen," I said. "You want some coffee?"

"That would be great," Rocco said.

I tossed him a notepad then got the coffee started. Chef Claire entered a few minutes later still half-asleep and wearing her bathrobe. Startled, she blinked when she saw us sitting around the kitchen island.

"Good morning," Chef Claire said, stifling a yawn.

"Morning," I said. "Chef Claire, this is Rocco. We're talking with him about doing the remodel to the downstairs bathroom."

"Hey," Chef Claire said, managing a small wave. "Nice to meet you."

"Hi," Rocco said, looking up from the piece of paper he was making notes on. "So, you're the famous chef everybody's talking about."

"So they tell me," Chef Claire said, trying to stifle a yawn and smile at the same time.

"You look beat. What time did you get home last night?" Josie said.

"Not until a little after two," she said, accepting my offer of a mug of coffee. "I should have been home by midnight, but I had to wait for Jackson to finish up."

I frowned and glanced at Josie. She shrugged and waited to hear more.

"Wait for Jackson to finish up what?" I said.

"I imagine it was all the usual police stuff. You know the drill. Make sure he got the situation deescalated, interview all the witnesses. We had a little problem in the bar," Chef Claire said.

"Oh, no," I said, shaking my head. "What happened?"

"Morrie and that woman came in for dinner," Chef Claire said. "And after they ate, they went to the bar for an after dinner drink and got into an argument."

"What woman are you talking about?" I said.

"Franny," Chef Claire said.

"She didn't shoot anybody did she?" Josie said.

"Nah," Rocco interjected, glancing up. "That's not Franny's style."

Then he refocused on the quote for the bathroom.

"You know Franny?" I said.

"Sure," Rocco said, tapping his pen on the granite. "Everybody who works, uh, worked for Jimmy knows who Franny is. And she's right near the top in the workplace safety manual. Item one; always wear your hardhat. Item two; know where Franny is at all times."

He smiled and glanced around, obviously waiting for a laugh. Then he shrugged and resumed his work.

"Inside joke I guess," he said.

"What were they arguing about?" I said.

"Jackson said they were both pretty short on specifics," Chef Claire said. "But it was probably something about Calducci."

"No doubt about that," Rocco said, not even bothering to look up.

"Are you going to join the conversation, or are you just going to dabble around the edges?" Josie said.

Rocco found her response funny, and he laughed hard. Then he put the pen down and placed his elbows on the island.

"Okay, I'll play," he said. "What do you want to know?"

His direct question caught me by surprise, and I paused to organize my thoughts before responding.

"Do you know Morrie?"

"Sure, everybody knows Morrie. I love the guy. It's just a pity that Jimmy had him in his pocket all those years."

"You're referring to the fact that Calducci was skimming thirty percent off the top of Morrie's business, right?"

"Gee, that's odd," Rocco said, his eyes narrowing as he glared at me. "I don't remember saying anything about Calducci skimming off the top of anything."

"Forget I mentioned it," I said.

"I hope I can," he said in a soft, low voice that sent chills up my spine.

"Okay, moving on," I said, recovering. "How about Franny? Are you willing to talk about her?"

"Sure, her I'll talk about," Rocco said. "What do you want to know?"

"What was her relationship with Calducci?" I said, sitting down at the island across from him.

"They were close," Rocco said. "Basically, they took care of each other."

"Took care of each other professionally… or personally?" I said, casually taking a sip of coffee.

"I imagine it was both," Rocco said. "But it wasn't any of my business, so I never really gave it much thought."

"But you must have wondered about the nature of their relationship at some point," I said.

Rocco chuckled and shook his head.

"What?" I said, mildly annoyed by his reaction.

"Lady, you need to stick to dogs because you make a lousy cop," Rocco said, laughing.

Josie snorted and sat down next to Rocco. Chef Claire headed for the shower leaving the three of us sitting at the island.

"What exactly did Franny do for Calducci?" I said.

"Pretty much anything Jimmy needed to be done," Rocco said. "Jimmy wasn't well-liked in a lot of circles, and having Franny around was a pretty solid insurance policy. She traveled everywhere with him, and was always by his side."

"Except for the other day when he died," Josie said.

"Yeah," Rocco said, nodding. "I have to admit that I've been wondering about that myself."

"What did Mrs. Calducci think about Franny and her husband?" I said.

"Dot?" Rocco whispered. He exhaled and gave us a sad smile. "I doubt if Dot even knew when Franny was in the same room with her. But that's not surprising since Dot barely knows where she is most of the time these days."

"The booze, right?" I said.

"Yeah, and it's really hard to watch it happen," he said. "At one time, Dot was an amazing woman."

"We heard that she and Calducci had some legendary fights," I said.

"You've heard a lot," Rocco said, his eyes narrowing again into a hard glare.

It had the same effect on me as the first time he'd done it.

"Look, you both seem like nice people," Rocco said. "Why on earth are you poking around into this mess?"

I glanced at Josie, and she nodded at me to go first.

"I guess you could say it's kind of a hobby," I said, immediately hating my answer. "And we've got a knack for it."

"A hobby? Lady, you might want to consider something a bit safer. Like hang-gliding," Rocco said. "You got a knack for it." He found that comment especially funny. When he stopped laughing, he turned serious and waited until he was sure I was paying attention. "You should leave this one to the people who are actually in the life to figure out."

"Sure, sure," I said, nodding. "You mentioned that it's a mess."

Rocco stared at me, then looked at Josie who shrugged.

"Slow learner," Josie said, taking a sip of coffee.

"I can see that," Rocco said, studying me closely. "It's a mess because Jimmy's death opens up a power vacuum that several people are going to want to fill."

"That makes sense," I said, then decided to push the conversation along. "So, who do you think killed Calducci?"

"Jimmy had a heart attack," Rocco said. "Who said anything about murder?"

"Well, Fatal Franny for one," I said.

Rocco chuckled and drained the last of his coffee.

"Yeah, I heard her speech at the funeral. She can be a real drama queen. That was classic Franny."

"She sounded pretty serious to me," I said.

"Me too," Josie said.

"I'm sure she was," Rocco said. "But whenever you hear Franny mouthing off in public, you don't have anything to worry about. It's when you don't hear her coming up behind you that's the problem."

"So, you don't think anybody killed Calducci?" I said.

"No, I didn't say that," Rocco said. "I just reminded you that he had a heart attack and then asked a question."

For some reason, I decided to continue digging deeper into the big hole I'd somehow managed to create for myself.

"The question sounded rhetorical to me," I said.

Rocco chuckled again and looked at Josie.

"Tenacious isn't she?" he said.

"I guess tenacious is a word for it," Josie said. "I couldn't help but notice the scar tissue. Did you used to box professionally?"

"No, only in prison," Rocco said. "I guess I was good enough to be called a pro, but you're pretty much forced to fight for free in there. But if it makes any difference, it was always in self-defense."

"Interesting," Josie said. "If you don't mind my asking, what were you in for?"

"Mainly breaking and entering. But that was a long time ago."

"B&E? Is that how you met Morrie?" I said.

Rocco stared at me open-mouthed.

"Lady, I don't know where you're getting all your information, but you need to stop," Rocco said. "Trust me. I'm doing you a favor telling you that."

"Sure, sure," I said, nodding. "And I appreciate that, Rocco. Just one more thing. We noticed four guys in our restaurant the day of the funeral who looked like they were definitely *in the business*. You wouldn't happen to know who they were, would you?"

"This conversation is over," Rocco said, focusing on the piece of paper in front of him.

We watched him make a few final notes, then he added up a list of numbers and slid the paper across the island. I glanced down at the total, then slid it toward Josie. She studied it, then nodded.

"That's a good number, Rocco," I said. "Very reasonable."

"One of us needs to be," he said.

"Funny," I said, scowling.

"Is it okay if I start in a couple of days?"

"Sure, that would be great," I said. "Thanks, Rocco. Maybe we'll see you around town before then."

"Yeah," he said, getting up from his stool. "Based on this conversation, that wouldn't surprise me at all."

He paused at the kitchen door and turned around.

"I just gave you some good advice. Do yourself a favor and try to take it."

He waved goodbye and let himself out. Josie collected our coffee mugs and put them in the dishwasher.

"What do you think?" I said.

"About what?"

"Should we put Rocco on the suspect list?"

"Didn't you already do that?" Josie said.

"No, I'm not sure about him yet," I said, frowning. "I'm torn."

"Well, let's hope it remains just a tear and we don't get ripped in half."

"You worry too much," I said.

"Yeah, I'm the problem here," Josie said, glancing at her watch. "I have a couple of exams and a minor surgery to take care of this morning. What time do you want to take the dogs out on the River?"

"How about three o'clock?"

"That works," Josie said. "Maybe we'll get lucky and not run into Howard and Franny."

"Aren't you curious?" I said.

"I was," Josie said. "But this one is starting to make me nervous, Suzy."

Chapter 13

We were on the boat just after three and on our way to the Lake of the Isles. Since it was mid-week, it was quiet when we arrived. Captain and Chloe jumped in for a swim, while Josie and I snacked and laughed while we watched their antics. Thirty minutes later they had tired themselves out, and we helped them climb back into the boat, doing our best to stay dry while they shook, then toweled them off. Both dogs were soon stretched out on the cushioned seats sound asleep.

I steered the boat toward Lover's Cove, a secluded area attached to Wellesley Island that was aptly named. The cove was quite small and easy to miss if you weren't paying attention. It contained several rocky outcrops dotted with cedar and pine trees that provided additional privacy to boaters looking to get away from it all and, more importantly for many of young people who came here, not be seen. Once inside the cove, a sense of tranquility always seemed to surround me, and it was easy to forget that this small inlet was still part of the mighty St. Lawrence that stretched over 700 miles.

I slowed the boat as we entered and I glanced over the side into the clear, shallow water. Chloe and Captain both woke and glanced around, apparently anticipating another opportunity to take a swim.

"It doesn't look like anybody else is here," Josie said. "But you were right, if I wanted some privacy, this would be the place to find it."

"That's right," I said. "You've never been here before."

"I haven't needed this kind of privacy in quite a while," Josie said, laughing.

"Tell me about it," I said, slowly inching the boat forward until I was sure there wasn't a boat tucked behind the first outcrop.

"If we do happen to bump into Howard and Franny, how do we explain us being here?" she said. "After all, the place is called Lover's Cove."

"Way ahead of you," I said, not taking my eyes off the shallow water we were idling through. "We came here so the dogs could swim in a safe, quiet spot."

"That should work," Josie said, nodding. "But what exactly are you hoping to find out?"

"I'm not really sure," I said, navigating away from a shoal near another of the outcrops.

"Well done, Sherlock," she said. "We came all the way out here, and you're not sure why?"

"I'd just like to get an idea why Franny agreed to go out with Howard in the first place," I said. "I still think it's because she wants to find out if Howard knows more about who robbed his pharmacy than he's letting on."

"And if he does, you think that Franny might have to do something about Howard?" Josie said.

"It has to be a possibility, right? If she's connected to Calducci's murder, and if Howard can identify the person who broke into his place, it probably wouldn't take much for the cops to connect the dots back to Franny."

"And you expect to be able to get a feel for what's going on just by watching the two of them interact with each other?" Josie said.

"Maybe."

"Or perhaps Franny will tip her hand in some way?" Josie said, a smile starting to form on her face.

"Maybe," I said, casually shrugging.

"You couldn't think of anything else to do, could you?" Josie said, laughing.

"Nope," I said.

"Unbelievable," she said. "Silly me. Here I thought you actually had a plan."

"I'm hoping a plan will emerge at some point," I said, catching a glimpse of something just ahead of us and pointing. "There it is."

The bow of Howard's runabout was poking out from behind one of the outcrops.

"Remember, Suzy," Josie said. "No sneaking up on them."

"Absolutely not," I said. "We'll let Captain and Chloe handle it."

I picked up a tennis ball, whistled, and then tossed the ball in the general direction of Howard's boat. Both dogs jumped off the transom and made a beeline for the ball. Their barking alone would have been enough to wake the dead, and it would certainly get the attention of Howard and Franny. But we didn't hear any sounds coming from the boat. I leaned over the side, eventually managed to extract the tennis ball from Captain's mouth, and threw it again. This time, it landed right next to Howard's boat, and Captain actually bumped against it while he battled Chloe for possession. The boat rocked, but we still didn't hear anything.

"Where the heck are they?" I said, staring at Howard's boat.

"I guess they could have gone for a walk," Josie said. "If they didn't mind getting their feet wet walking to shore."

"Yeah," I said, frowning. "It's possible. But it seems odd they'd leave the comfort of the boat to walk through that stand of trees. It's pretty thick back there."

"Maybe Franny wanted more privacy before she, well, you know," Josie said.

"No, there were too many people who knew they were going out on the boat," I said. "And remember what Rocco said, if she were going to shoot somebody, they'd never hear her coming."

"Maybe Howard got a little too *hands-on* with her," Josie said. "After all, this is Howard we're talking about."

"I can see that happening," I said. "But if he did, wouldn't Franny have popped him before he could even get off the boat?"

"Yeah, probably," Josie said. "She does seem to have a bit of a quick temper."

"Well, let's check it out," I said, inching the boat forward until we were alongside Howard's.

Josie tied them together, and we glanced around Howard's empty boat. A picnic basket and a cooler sat on the floor near the stern. A couple of blankets, still folded neatly, were stacked on one of the cushioned seats. I stepped onto Howard's boat and ran my hand over the outboard motor.

"The engine's cold," I said, continuing to look around. "And the keys are in the ignition."

"What do you think?" Josie said.

"I think your theory about them taking a walk is all we've got to work with at the moment," I said, climbing back onto our boat and sitting down to remove my shoes.

"You're going to go barefoot?" Josie said, frowning.

"Only until we reach shore," I said. "I hate walking in wet, squishy sneakers."

"Good thinking," Josie said, removing her running shoes. "How cold do you think the water is?"

"Cold enough to get your attention," I said, glancing over the side. "But it's only about a hundred feet to shore."

"That sounds like a long way," she said.

"Not really," I said, sliding into the water holding my shoes in one hand and a towel in the other. "It'll only seem like a long way. Ooh, now that's cold."

Josie followed me into the water, gasped, then whistled at the dogs who continued to swim and wrestle with each other over the tennis ball. Captain and Chloe spotted us in the water and made a beeline for us. We waded toward shore, shoes in hand, and, gradually, the water got even shallower until it barely reached our calves. I stepped onto shore, sat down on a stretch of rock and dried my feet. I tossed the towel to Josie, put my sneakers back on, then unsuccessfully tried to duck the spray Captain and Chloe's shakes produced.

"You just had to stand next to me and do that, didn't you?" I said.

Chloe barked once and stared at me, waiting to hear what was next on our agenda. I stood and looked around trying to remember the area from my younger days.

"It doesn't look like a place for a quiet walk in the woods," Josie said, glancing around. "It's even thicker than it looks from the boat."

"If I remember correctly, I think it opens up a bit once you get through this section," I said, starting to make my way through the cedar and pines.

"At least it smells good," Josie said, pushing branches away from her face.

113

"Just try not to get any pine tar in your hair," I said. "It's a total pain to get out."

"Remind me again why I'm out here in the forest when I could be home relaxing?" she said over the sound of snapping tree branches as she pushed forward.

"Because we're worried about Howard," I said.

"Try again," Josie said.

"Because I can't help snooping?"

"There you go."

We continued to push forward through the trees and, eventually, things did open up. We roamed around the rocks and patches of grass in a couple different directions but didn't see anything other than a mother Mallard and her ducklings that were trailing behind her as she made her way toward the River. Captain and Chloe both saw the ducks and stared at them with their heads cocked as if they couldn't believe what they were seeing.

Then Josie and I called out for Howard and Franny in loud voices. We waited, repeated our calls, then gave up.

"This is really strange," I said. "Where on earth could they be?"

"I have no idea," Josie said. "But I'm getting eaten alive so let's get out of here."

The mosquitos were definitely on the prowl, and I wasn't about to argue. We made our way back through the trees, removed our shoes, and waded back to the boat. We helped the dogs onboard, dried off, and I sat down to think.

"If they're not on the boat and they're not on shore, where the heck are they?" I said.

"I guess they could be *in* the water," Josie said.

"Drowned?" I said, shaking my head. "I don't see that. Howard's been a River Rat since he was a kid, and I can't see him doing something stupid like falling in and drowning."

"Well, they sure wouldn't have gone for a romantic swim," Josie said. "That water is freezing cold."

"The only other place they could be is on another boat," I said. "But that seems highly unlikely."

"Unless they were forced onto another boat," I said.

"You mean like they were kidnapped?" Josie said. "That's even weirder than the idea about them going for a romantic swim."

"Yeah, it is strange," I said. "But if somebody had Fatal Franny on their radar and wanted to take her out, it wouldn't be that hard to follow Howard's boat out here. Actually, this is a good spot to do something like that. It's pretty remote, and the chances of being seen are very small."

"And since Howard just happened to be along for the ride," Josie said. "I can see the possibility of whoever was looking for Franny would be forced to take him out, too."

"Yeah, wrong place at the wrong time," I said. "Poor Howard."

I grabbed my phone and placed the call. I put it on speaker and waited. It was answered on the third ring.

"This is Jackson."

"Hey, it's me."

"Hi, Suzy. What's shaking?"

"Uh, I think we need your help," I said.

"Okay. Where are you?"

"Josie and I are at Lover's Cove," I said.

"And you want some male company," Jackson said, laughing. "Give me twenty minutes."

"Funny," I said.

"Hey, Josie," Jackson said.

"Hi, Jackson. How are you doing?"

"Probably better than I'm going to be after this call. What's up?"

"Howard's boat is here, but there's no sight of him or his date," I said.

"His date? Man, that guy never stops, does he?" Jackson said. "You'd think that between running his pharmacy and being mayor he'd have plenty of things to keep him busy."

"Yeah, one would think," I said, waiting for the question.

"Who was his date?" Jackson said.

"Fatal Franny," I said.

"The shooter who worked for Calducci? What the heck is Howard doing with her?" Jackson said. "Never mind. Dumb question."

"Can you get out here?" I said.

"Yeah, I was about to knock off for the rest of the day and take Sluggo out on the boat," he said. "I'll just bring the police boat instead."

"Bring Sluggo with you," Josie said. "Captain and Chloe are here."

"Will do," he said. "Are there any signs of trouble?"

"No, nothing," I said. "We even walked the shoreline."

"That does seem strange," Jackson said. "Where exactly are you?"

"We're tucked inside the last outcrop on the right," I said.

"Okay, stay put for the next half hour," Jackson said.

I slid the phone back into my pocket and sat back down. Then I noticed Josie climbing into Howard's boat.

"Where are you going?" I said.

"I thought I'd take a quick look at what's inside that picnic basket," Josie said.

"You think you're going to find some clues in there?" I said, laughing.

"The heck with clues, I'm starving."

Chapter 14

While we waited for Jackson, we dug into Howard's picnic basket and discovered a bag of brownies from Paterson's bakery. Since they were one of our personal favorites, we made short work of them as the dogs jumped back into the water for another swim. Both dogs spotted the police boat approaching and started barking excitedly when they saw Sluggo in the seat next to Jackson.

Despite our concerns about what might have happened to Howard and Franny, we laughed at the sight of the bulldog standing on his back legs with his front paws pressing against the windshield. We helped Captain and Chloe back into the boat, got drenched again from their shakes, then accepted Sluggo from Jackson and put him down next to Captain and Chloe. Soon, they were rolling around on the floor of the boat oblivious to our presence. Jackson tied his boat to ours, then climbed onto Howard's boat and began a quick review.

"Nothing's out of place, no sign of a struggle, no blood," Jackson said, eventually. "I got nothing. Where the heck did they go?"

"They either had to get on another boat," Josie said. "Or they went in the water, right?"

Jackson frowned and scanned the shoreline in both directions.

"I guess," he said. "Are you sure they aren't on shore?"

"I can't be positive," I said. "But we gave it a good look. And we called their names several times. I doubt if they heard us they would have decided to hide."

"Why not? I've used that strategy before with you," Jackson said, laughing. "It's actually one of my go-to moves."

"Funny," I said.

"Okay, I guess I need to get some search and rescue folks out here. If they're in the water, we'll know soon enough. The current only runs one way, and it would keep their bodies here in the cove."

Jackson placed a call, and we waited quietly until he finished.

"They're on their way," he said. "We've only got a couple of hours of daylight left, so I'm not sure how much we'll be able to get done today. You know, I just don't see Howard drowning. He's too good on the River to do some stupid like that."

"Then that leaves another boat, right?" Josie said.

"Probably," Jackson said. "But why would Howard leave his here? You know how protective of that boat he is."

"He must have been forced to leave it here," I said.

"By people looking for Fatal Franny?" Jackson said.

"I doubt if it was anybody wanting to hurt Howard," I said. "He's a total hound dog, but he's a good guy and pretty harmless."

"Unless he slept with the wrong woman," Josie said.

"I hadn't thought of that," Jackson said, nodding. "I guess that's a possibility."

"And Fatal Franny just stood by and let it happen?" I said. "Nah, I'm not buying that. It has to be connected to Calducci."

"If that's the case, then I'm leaning toward Morrie the Meat Guy," Jackson said.

"No way," Josie said, shaking her head. "He's such a sweet old man."

"Josie, the guy has a criminal background and spent years working for Calducci," Jackson said. "And if you would have seen the look in his eyes at the restaurant when he was arguing with Fatal Franny, you might have a different opinion."

I'd completely forgotten to ask Jackson about the details of Morrie's argument with Franny at the restaurant.

I must be slipping.

"What were they fighting about?" I said.

"Well, given their attitude about cooperating with cops, they were pretty short on the specifics. But it sounded like they got into it over percentages of something and about who got what."

"Morrie's business," I said. "Calducci was skimming thirty percent off the top."

"You think Fatal Franny is trying to take over?" Josie said.

"It's possible," I said. "Maybe Morrie was pushing back and trying to negotiate a lower percentage."

"Or trying to get out from underneath the whole thing," Josie said. "I know I would."

"And Calducci's death would be the perfect time to try," I said.

"Yeah, it would," Jackson said. "But it's not easy to get away from those people's clutches. Once they've got their hooks into somebody, they tend to hold on pretty tight."

"And you think Morrie followed Howard out here and somehow managed to get the drop on Fatal Franny?" I said, frowning.

"Managed to get the drop?" Josie said, laughing. "Keep it up, and I'm going to have to hide the remote."

"You know what I mean," I said, making a face at her. "But how would Morrie do that all by himself?"

"Element of surprise?" Jackson said.

"Or maybe he had help," Josie said.

"Yes, he might have had help," I said, my mind racing. "Dot and Pee Wee?"

"If Franny was trying to take over Calducci's operation, that makes some sense," Jackson said.

"Assuming that Dot is interested in running it," Josie said. "All she seems interested in these days is her next cocktail."

"And Pee Wee," I said.

"Yeah, we can't forget about him," Josie said.

"Dot and Pee Wee are an item?" Jackson said.

"So it appears," Josie said.

"They're an odd combination for a couple," Jackson said.

"If it's not Dot and Pee Wee," I said. "I wonder if it could be one or more of those four guys we saw Franny talking to at the restaurant?"

"I did some digging into who those guys are," Jackson said. "They're the four guys who reported directly to Calducci."

"And one of them could be moved up to run things?" I said.

"Apparently, that's the word on the street," Jackson said. "But nobody seems to know how it's going to play out. Everything seems to be in limbo at the moment."

"Again, that's the perfect time for everybody to make their move," I said. "I just can't believe that Morrie is involved. But if he is, who else could he be working with?"

"Maybe a longtime friend," Josie said, staring at me.

"You mean like a certain construction guy?" I said.

"Exactly," Josie said.

"Who are you talking about?" Jackson said.

"A guy who's been working on our expansion project at the Inn," I said. "His name is Rocco."

"Short guy with tons of muscle whose face looks like it went ten rounds with an immersion blender?"

"Yeah, that's him," I said. "Do you know him?"

"Only by reputation," Jackson said. "He's a scary dude. I'm glad you're almost finished with the expansion. From what I've heard, he's a guy you don't want hanging around."

I glanced at Josie who seemed to have a grimace frozen on her face. Then she pointed a finger in the direction of home.

"If you don't need us to stick around," I said. "I think we'll get going, Jackson."

"No, that's fine. I'll let you know if we find anything," he said. "And if Howard or Franny do happen to surface, give me a call."

"Will do," I said, starting the engine.

"Hey, before I forget," Jackson said. "Chef Claire's birthday is coming up. Are you guys planning a party?"

"Yes, we're going to close the restaurant on that Monday and have it there," I said. "The invitations are going out in a couple of days."

"What a great idea," Jackson said. "What are you guys getting her?"

"We're still debating," Josie said. "How about you?"

"I can't make up my mind," Jackson said. "But it has to be something special. I think I might be running out of time when it comes to Chef Claire."

He stared at us and tried to read our expressions. We both did our best to give him a blank stare in return. Apparently, they weren't quite blank enough.

"What is it? You guys know something, don't you?" Jackson said, glancing back and forth at us. "What did Chef Claire tell you?"

"Nothing, really," I said.

"Just the usual," Josie said. "You know, she's having trouble making up her mind. Stuff like that."

"Gee, why don't I believe you?" Jackson said, maintaining his stare.

"Because you're a cop, Jackson," I said. "You're trained not to believe what people tell you."

"Uh-huh," he said, giving us the evil eye. "Then it sounds like my birthday present needs to be extra special. The diamond tennis bracelet I gave her for Christmas was a total homerun."

"More diamonds? Just give her something from the heart, Jackson," Josie said. "That's all Chef Claire would want you to do."

"And try not to overthink it," I said.

"You should be able to handle that," Josie deadpanned.

"Not funny," Jackson said.

"Disagree."

Josie gently woke Sluggo, picked him up, and handed him to Jackson. Chloe and Captain continued to snore their way through a deep sleep. We waved to Jackson and slowly made our way out of the cove.

"Strange days," Josie said.

"Indeed."

"You worried about letting Rocco inside the house?" she said.

"Actually, I'm not," I said. "Are you?"

"Maybe a little," Josie said. "What if Rocco hasn't gone quite as straight as he told us?"

"He wouldn't be the first criminal we've come in contact with, right?"

"No," Josie said. "But that doesn't necessarily make me feel any better."

We reached deep water, and I opened the throttle. The bow rose, then the boat planed, and we headed for home at a brisk thirty miles an hour.

"Besides, what reason could Rocco possibly have to hurt us?" I said over the roar of the engine.

"Probably the same reason somebody would have to hurt Howard," Josie said.

Chapter 15

The next morning we swung by the restaurant to have an early breakfast with Chef Claire. We'd barely seen her in days, and it still seemed strange not having her around the house in the evening. She seemed tired but happy as she refilled our coffee.

"How are the pancakes?" she said, cutting into her stack.

"Amazing," I said, munching on a slice of bacon.

Josie tried to speak through a mouthful of food, then gave up and settled for a vigorous nod.

"Are you guys really sure you want to close the restaurant just for my birthday party?"

"Absolutely," I said. "And it's a Monday. You said it's our slowest night."

"Yes, it's our slowest, but it's not really slow. And I've already had to turn down several people who wanted reservations for that night," Chef Claire said.

"Invite them to the party," Josie said.

"Now, there's a thought," Chef Claire said, turning around in her chair. "Hey, Morrie. You're here early today."

Morrie smiled and waved as he walked across the kitchen. He accepted Chef Claire's invitation to have coffee and sat down at the chef's table next to Josie.

"Good morning, ladies," he said. "And congratulations on the restaurant. Everybody is buzzing about it."

"Thanks, Morrie. But it's all Chef Claire," I said. "Why the early start? It's still dark out."

"I have a couple of things to take care of this afternoon, so it's going to be a short day of work," Morrie said, taking a sip of coffee. "And I thought I'd swing by as soon as I hit town. Chef Claire said she's making something that needs to get in the oven this morning. So you're my first stop."

"What time did you leave Rochester this morning?" Josie said, pushing her empty plate away.

"Just before three," he said. "And even then I was late getting on the road. I didn't even get a chance to take check the truck to make sure my guys got all the orders right."

"Hey, Morrie," Josie said. "Would you happen to have an extra Bresaola we could buy from you? I'd love to have some at the house."

"Why don't you just move your bed into the walk-in?" Chef Claire said, laughing as she reached for the plate of bacon.

"Don't worry," I said. "She's been thinking about it. Which one is the Bresaola?"

"That's the deep red cured meat that comes on the antipasto. But I'm thinking about adding as its own appetizer," Chef Claire said. "It's an air-dried beef. I like to slice it razor-thin and serve it with olive oil, drizzled with lemon juice and capers. It's yummy."

"This girl sure does know her food," Morrie said, nodding at Chef Claire before glancing down at his IPad. "I'm not sure if

I have an extra one, Josie. Let's see. I have orders for two of them today. So why don't you go have a look in the back of the truck? If there's more than two in there, feel free to grab one."

"I'll be right back," Josie said, hopping to her feet and jogging toward the door.

"You'd think she was going to Disneyland," Morrie said, laughing as he watched Josie cross the kitchen.

"For her, the back of your truck is Disneyland," Chef Claire said.

We made small talk for the next few minutes, then we stopped when we saw Josie standing in the doorway with a stunned look on her face.

"What's the problem?" I said, laughing. "No Bresaola?"

"Uh, you guys need to come with me," Josie said, her voice trembling.

"What on earth is the matter?" I said, walking toward her.

"You need to see it for yourself," Josie said, tears rolling down her face.

We walked outside and saw Morrie's refrigerated truck parked near the loading dock. Josie had left the back door open. Josie hung back while Morrie, Chef Claire and I approached the truck and peered inside.

"Oh, no," I whispered.

I squeezed my eyes shut hoping to erase what I'd just seen from my memory.

"Wow. Is that who I think it is?" Chef Claire said.

"It certainly is," Morrie whispered.

I opened my eyes and took another look at the body. Fatal Franny was hanging from a meat hook and gently swaying back and forth. Her eyes, unlike mine, were wide open and she had a single bullet hole in the middle of her forehead.

"She and Howard disappeared yesterday afternoon when they were on the River," I said.

"Really?" Chef Claire said, glancing back inside the truck. "I don't see Howard in there."

"I wonder who shot her?" Chef Claire said.

"That's a good question," Morrie said, stunned and staring at the body. "But I've got a better one."

"How did she end up hanging in your truck?" I said.

"That's the one," Morrie said, exhaling loudly as he rubbed his forehead. "This is bad."

"Especially after you and Franny had that argument in the restaurant," Chef Claire said.

"Yup," Morrie said.

"Do you have an alibi for yesterday afternoon?" I said.

"Not a good one," Morrie said.

"So, what do we do now?" Chef Claire said.

"Well, you guys need to call the cops," Morrie said. "I'm going to call my lawyer."

Ten minutes later, Jackson and Freddie, our local medical examiner, arrived in separate cars. Morrie was on the phone with his lawyer when Jackson approached, and Morrie gestured for

Jackson to wait for him to finish the call. Jackson stood nearby as Morrie continued his conversation, then he looked over at us sitting on the edge of the loading dock.

"Any word from Howard?" Jackson said.

"No," I said. "You heard anything?"

Jackson shook his head. He wasn't in the mood to wait any longer and motioned for Morrie to hurry up. Morrie finished his call, slid his phone back into his pocket, and looked at Jackson.

"What do you need to know, Jackson?" Morrie said.

"Gee, Morrie, where do I start?" Jackson said, glancing over his shoulder at the truck. "Let's go with how is it possible you didn't know she was in there?"

"Like I told the ladies earlier, I got a late start this morning and didn't have time to check the back of the truck."

"Is that unusual?" Jackson said.

"Not really," Morrie said. "My guys are really good about getting all the trucks organized for the next day's deliveries."

"Okay," Jackson said. "But I've been wondering something, Morrie, why would a guy who owns a successful restaurant supply business still be driving a truck and making deliveries?"

Morrie frowned and looked down at the ground.

I had to give Jackson credit. It was a very good question and something I'd also wondered about.

"I really don't want to answer that, Jackson," Morrie said, finally managing to make eye contact.

"Can I ask you why?" Jackson said.

"Because it's not relevant to this situation," Morrie said.

"Morrie, there's a woman with a bullet hole in her head hanging from a meat hook in your truck," Jackson said. "Until we learn a bit more, I'm afraid that everything should be considered relevant."

"I'm sorry, Jackson," Morrie said. "For now, I'm not going to answer that question."

"Okay," Jackson said, studying Morrie's face. "We'll get back to that one later. Where were you yesterday afternoon between two and six?"

"Let's say I was in that truck," Morrie said. "I left Clay Bay around two-thirty and drove back to Rochester."

"Isn't it a bit strange for you to make deliveries here two days in a row?" Jackson said.

"Jackson's on his game today," I whispered to Josie.

"Yeah, he must have figured out a way to get his mind off Chef Claire and back on his work," Josie whispered, then winced. "Ow, that hurt."

"Good," Chef Claire said, glaring at Josie. "Don't start."

"Okay, okay," Josie said, rubbing her upper arm. "There's no need for violence."

"It's a little late to start worrying about that, isn't it?" I said, nodding at the truck.

"What can I tell you, Jackson?" Morrie said. "It's been a bad week at work. A couple of my guys were up here for Jimmy's funeral, so my warehouse was short-staffed. One of my new guys got several orders screwed up, and I had to make a second run to make sure folks like Chef Claire had everything they needed."

"And even after your orders were wrong earlier in the week, you didn't feel the need to check the truck before you headed out this morning?" Jackson said.

"I told you. I was running late," Morrie said. "And my guys who attended the funeral are back at work. And I trust them to get things right the first time."

"Did you make any stops on the way home yesterday?" Jackson said.

"No, I drove straight through," Morrie said, shaking his head.

"Didn't stop to grab a bite to eat?"

"No."

"Maybe you stopped to go to the bathroom," Jackson said.

"Nope."

"You didn't stop to get gas?" Jackson said.

"No, I had half a tank," Morrie said. "I didn't gas up until this morning when I got into town."

"Okay," Jackson said, glancing at Freddie who was still inside the truck. "I'm sorry, Morrie, but I'm going to need to take you in."

"Yes, I'm sure you do, Jackson," Morrie said.

"And you're going to have to start answering a whole bunch of questions," Jackson said, gently pulling Morrie by the elbow toward the police car.

"I know, Jackson," Morrie said. "And I'll be more than happy to do that as soon as my lawyer gets here."

Morrie reached the car and started to climb into the back seat. Then he stopped and looked at us with a sad expression.

"I'm sorry, ladies," Morrie said. "I have no idea how Franny ended up in there. And I hope you believe me that I would never do anything that might harm you or your restaurant."

"Take care, Morrie," I said, giving him a small wave. "Let us know if you need anything."

We watched Jackson drive away and hopped down off the loading dock just as Freddie was climbing out of the back of Morrie's truck.

"Good morning, guys," Freddie said, removing his latex gloves. "Hi, Chef Claire. You're looking beautiful today."

"Thanks, Freddie," Chef Claire said. "I haven't seen you around in a couple of days."

"After our last conversation, I thought it would be a good idea to give you a bit of space," Freddie said.

"Interesting" Josie said, grinning. "Care to share any details?"

"No," Freddie said.

"Absolutely not," Chef Claire said.

"Spoilsports," Josie said in mock anger.

"And I had to go out of town," Freddie said. "I did some shopping for your birthday."

"Freddie, please don't go overboard," Chef Claire said.

"Don't worry," Freddie said. "All I'm going to say is that I decided to go big. You're either going to be blown away by it, or hate me forever."

"Will it go well with the diamond bracelet you got her for Christmas?" Josie said, grinning.

Freddie thought about it, then nodded.

"Yeah, I think the two will go very well together," he said.

"What have you done, Freddie?" Chef Claire said.

"You'll see," Freddie said, beaming at her.

Chef Claire looked at me with pleading eyes. I got the message and switched topics.

"What's the story with Fatal Franny?" I said.

"One shot in the middle of the forehead," Freddie said. "And unless I'm wrong, which I rarely am, she was shot with her own gun."

He held up a sealed plastic bag that contained a large pistol.

"Somebody shot her with her own gun?" I said. "How the heck did they get it away from her?"

"Probably by pointing another even bigger gun at her," Freddie said.

"You think there's a message in that?" I said.

"You mean, apart from '*Bang, you're dead*'?" Freddie said, chuckling.

"That's the sort of thing I've been talking about, Freddie," Chef Claire said, giving him a hard stare. "That's morbid."

"I'm sorry," Freddie said, chastised. Then he looked at me. "What sort of message are you talking about?"

"I'm just wondering if somebody was out for revenge," I said. "And the thought of using the same gun on Franny that she used to shoot somebody else might have been too tempting to resist."

"You mean like some weird ironic twist of fate?" Freddie said, frowning.

"Maybe," I said, then realized the theory had sounded much better when it was still rolling around in my head. "Nah, forget it."

"How long before you can get the body out of there?" Chef Claire said.

"It won't be long. As soon as I can get her bagged and tagged," Freddie said, then he paused when he saw Chef Claire wince. "Sorry. Why do you want to know?"

"Because I've got a couple hundred pounds of meat and cheese I need to get out of that truck," Chef Claire said. "And I'm sure not going to do it while she's still there."

"You mean while she's still *hanging around*?" Josie deadpanned.

"You're worse than him," Chef Claire snapped.

"You're still going to use the stuff from today's delivery?" I said, nodding at the truck.

"Sure," Chef Claire said. "Why not?"

"Because it's been sitting in there with a dead body," I said.

"It's all boxed and wrapped tight," Chef Claire said. "She didn't bleed all over the prime rib did she?"

"Now who's being morbid?" Freddie said. "No, she stopped bleeding long before she was put in the truck."

"There you go," Chef Claire said, glancing at me.

"Uh, no offense, Chef Claire," I said. "But I think I just might have dinner at home tonight."

"Good call," Josie said.

Chapter 16

We headed back to the Inn, and I went directly to the condo area to check on Oslo. We'd started a daily exercise program with him that consisted of rolling a ball across the floor and studying him as he retrieved it and dropped it at my feet. His balance was good, and he seemed alert, although he did tire easily. I stopped after ten minutes, waited for him to settle in my lap, and called my mother.

"Hi, Mom."

"Hello, darling. Any word from Howard yet?"

"No, but there has been a development," I said.

I gave her the overview about what had happened to Fatal Franny and answered her questions the best I could.

"That's dreadful," my mother said. "Did Jackson arrest Morrie?"

"I don't think he's actually arrested him yet, at least he hadn't earlier. But he did take him in for questioning."

"Poor man. But I knew that if he hung around town long enough, he was going to get in trouble," she said.

"What are you talking about, Mom?"

"Nothing, darling. I'm just babbling. Look, I need to run. You can tell me the rest of it at dinner tonight."

"Uh, Mom," I said. "I think I'm going to pass on dinner tonight."

"What's wrong? Aren't you feeling well?"

"I'm fine, Mom," I said. "I guess you could say that this is more about prevention."

"As usual, darling, I don't have a clue what you're talking about," my mother said, laughing. "Oh, well, your loss."

"Oh, Mom."

"Yes, darling?"

"You might want to go with the sea bass."

I helped Oslo get comfortable on his bed then headed for the reception area. We were busy, but Sammy and Jill seemed to have everything handled, so I headed for one of the exam rooms where I found Josie removing the last of several porcupine quills from a black Lab's tongue. The dog's owner was cringing and whining louder than his dog.

"Hey, Chester," I said, gently stroking the dog's head. "How the heck did you manage to get them inside your mouth?"

"He's been chasing the porcupine for a couple of weeks," the owner said. "This morning he managed to sneak up from behind, and he nipped at it."

"I doubt he'll be doing that again," Josie said, carefully working a small pair of pliers onto the quill. "Will you, Chester?"

The dog thumped its tail and appeared to be embarrassed more than anything else. Josie ran her finger along the dog's tongue, took one final look, then stepped back and removed her latex gloves.

"There you go," Josie said. "Good as new. But his mouth is probably going to be a bit tender so you might want to lay off giving him kibble for a day or two. Try some chicken and maybe some cooked carrots. Or some scrambled eggs."

"He'll like that. Won't you Chester?" the owner said.

I doubted if Chester's mind was on food at the moment, but I let it pass without comment.

"Anything else I need to do, Josie?" the owner said.

"No, he'll be fine," Josie said, patting the dog. "Just try to stick to the squirrels, Chester."

Josie lifted the dog off the exam table and set him down on the floor. We waved goodbye as they left and we headed for my office. Josie stretched out on the couch and groaned when Captain jumped up and draped himself on top of her.

"He's hit ninety pounds," Josie said, rubbing the Newfie's massive head.

"And he still has a long way to go," I said. "Oslo did great this morning."

"Good," Josie said. "Tomorrow we'll give the smaller bandage a shot. But if starts scratching at it, we'll probably have to put a cone on him."

"I hate doing that," I said.

"Yeah, I know. But it sure beats him ripping his stitches out."

I decided to change the subject to one that had been nagging at me.

"Why do you think Morrie is still making deliveries?" I said.

"Who knows?" Josie said. "Maybe money's tight. After all, Calducci was skimming thirty percent off the top."

"Yeah, that could be it," I said, nodding.

"Or maybe Morrie likes interacting with his customers. You know, make sure they're all happy with his product line," Josie said, unwrapping a bite-sized from a fresh bag.

"That could be handled over the phone," I said, waving her offer of the bag away.

"Maybe he just likes being in the area this time of year," Josie said. "Does he fish?"

"I wouldn't have a clue," I said. "I was wondering if Morrie might have a *friend* in town."

"Friend, as in girlfriend?"

"He is a widower," I said. "And he wouldn't answer Jackson's question about why he was still making deliveries. It seemed like an easy enough question to answer."

"But Morrie has a criminal past, remember? And I imagine he doesn't like sharing any more than he has to with the cops," Josie said. "Are you thinking that if he does have a girlfriend, it might have something to do with what happened to Calducci or Fatal Franny?"

"No," I said. "I'm just being nosy."

Josie snorted.

"So what do you think about all this?" Josie said.

"I'm pretty lost at the moment," I said. "But I still think it has to revolve around the question of who's going to control Calducci's operation."

"Well, getting Fatal Franny out of the way would have to be a good start," Josie said.

"Yeah, but why would anybody try to frame Morrie?"

"Maybe someone is trying to scare him," Josie said. "You know, keep him in line."

"And keep him paying the thirty percent," I said.

"Exactly," Josie said, sitting up. "You're getting too heavy for this, Captain."

"I don't think he agrees with you," I said, laughing as I watched the dog reposition himself onto Josie's lap. "It's pretty obvious Morrie didn't have a clue she was hanging in his truck."

"No, I'm sure he didn't. And he certainly wouldn't have suggested that I should take a look inside," Josie said, then she sat quietly and stared off into the distance.

"What is it?" I said.

"It's nothing," she said. "I was just really looking forward to having some of that Bresaola."

Chapter 17

I was sound asleep when my phone buzzed just after midnight. Since good news rarely arrives over the phone at that time of night, I rolled over, managed to turn a light on, and answered it on the fourth ring.

"This is Suzy," I said, sleepily rubbing Chloe's head who seemed even less happy about being woken up than I was.

"Hello, darling."

"Mom, are you okay?" I said, sitting up in bed.

"I'm fine, darling," she whispered. "But I thought you'd want to know that Howard was just admitted to the hospital."

"Really?" I said, rubbing my forehead as I tried to process that bit of news. "What happened to him?"

"It looks like he was attacked," my mother said.

"By who?"

"It's too soon to know any of the details, darling. Dr. Wilbur is in with him now, and I imagine he's going to give Howard something to help him sleep. We should hear more in the morning."

"Is Jackson there?" I said, swinging my legs over the edge of the bed.

"He's on his way," she said. "I'm sorry to call you this late, but I thought you'd want to know. Not that there's anything you can do for *him* at the moment."

I smiled when I caught her emphasis on *him*.

"Would you feel better if I came down, Mom?"

"Well, that's your decision, darling," my mother said. "But since you're up…"

"I'll get there as soon as I can, Mom," I said, climbing out of bed.

"I'll be waiting outside Howard's room, darling," she said. "Dreadful situation. Simply dreadful."

"See you soon, Mom."

I swapped out my pajamas for a pair of sweats and a tee shirt. I took a quick look in the mirror and decided that a baseball cap was preferable to a lengthy hair brushing session. I pulled my hair back into a ponytail and inserted it through the opening in the back of the hat, then washed and dried my face.

"Close enough," I said to the mirror.

Chloe, anticipating an adventure, hopped off the bed and sat waiting by the door. I headed down the hall and knocked on Josie's door. Captain woofed once, then I heard Josie stir.

"Yeah?" Josie said. "Is everything okay?"

"Sorry to wake you up, but Howard just got admitted to the hospital, and I thought you'd want to know," I said through the door. "I'm going to head over to keep my Mom company. You want to come?"

"Sure," Josie said, "Give me five minutes."

"I'll make coffee," I said. "I'm sure the cafeteria is closed, and that vending machine stuff is horrid.

"Good call," Josie said, then I heard her start laughing. "No, Captain. Give me my sneaker."

I headed for the kitchen and started the coffee. I sat down and stared at the coffeemaker as it gurgled and slowly began to brew. A few minutes later, Josie entered and sat down next to me at the kitchen island.

"Don't you know a watched coffeemaker never brews?" Josie said.

"I don't think that's how that saying goes," I said, yawning.

"What happened to Howard?" she said, leaning back in her chair as Captain placed his two front paws on her lap.

"My Mom said it was too soon to tell," I said.

I got up, filled two travel mugs with coffee, then poured the rest of the pot into a thermos.

"You're such a good daughter," Josie said, nodding at the thermos.

"I have my moments," I said, securing the top of the thermos.

We said goodbye to the dogs, then headed down the steps to my SUV. The drive to the hospital took less than ten minutes, and I parked in front, and we headed inside. As promised, my mother was sitting outside Howard's room staring forlornly at the cup of vending machine coffee in her hand. Jackson was sitting next to her, and he stood when he saw us approaching.

"Hey, guys," Jackson said, dragging two chairs closer.

"Hi, Jackson," I said, handing the thermos to my mother, then hugging him.

"You're a lifesaver, darling," my mother said, opening the thermos.

"So, what happened?" I said to Jackson.

"It's pretty strange, and we're short on details since we haven't had a chance to talk to Howard yet," Jackson said. "Somebody on Wellesley Island noticed his body on the side of the road and called 911. The paramedics found Howard semi-conscious and babbling about being abducted. It looks like he was beaten up, and he's got a ton of cuts and scratches. If he was trying to escape from where you found his boat that could be where he got scratched up. Some of the areas around that shoreline are pretty thick."

I nodded. Jackson wasn't going to get any argument from me about that.

I saw a look of sadness on Jackson's face, and I caught Josie's eye and nodded my head at our chief of police. Josie glanced at him over the top of her coffee cup and frowned, then shrugged back at me.

"Are you okay, Jackson?" I said.

"What? Oh, yeah, I'm fine," he said softly.

I decided he wasn't in the mood to chitchat, so I changed topics.

"What did you decide to do with Morrie?" I said.

"Him?" Jackson said, almost spitting the word out. "We let him go tonight."

"You didn't have enough to arrest him?" I said.

"No," Jackson said. "Not at the moment. But don't worry, I'm going to keep looking."

His eyes had turned dark, and he sat rigid in his chair. My mother looked around and shifted nervously in her seat.

"Okay, guys," I said, glancing back and forth at them. "What's going on?"

"Nothing, darling."

"Just let it go, Suzy," Jackson said.

Josie snorted.

"Yeah, good luck with that, Jackson," she said, laughing.

"Josie, please," my mother said.

"What on earth is the matter with you two?" I said, my voice rising a notch.

Jackson stared at me, then exhaled loudly and nodded.

"Okay, I'm sure you're going to hear all about it soon enough," Jackson said. "I finally got an answer to the question of why Morrie is still making deliveries up here."

"He has a girlfriend in town, right?" I said.

"How on earth did you know that?" Jackson said.

"I kind of just put two and two together," I said, glancing at my mother who was unable to make eye contact.

Then a thought flashed through my head.

"Mom?" I said, staring at her wide-eyed.

"What?" my mother said, then scrunched up her face at me. "Me and Morrie? No, of course not."

"No, it's not your mom, Suzy," Jackson whispered. "It's mine."

"What? No way," I said, stunned by the news. "Morrie the Meat Guy and your mother?"

"Yeah," Jackson whispered.

"But your mom and dad have always been the role model of a happy marriage," Josie said.

"I guess times change," Jackson whispered.

Jackson wiped his eyes with the back of his sleeve, then stood up.

"I'll be back in a minute," he said, slowly walking down the hall.

I focused on my mother.

"That's what you were referring to when you said you knew that Morrie would eventually get into trouble if he kept hanging around town," I said.

"Yes, darling."

"How long have you known about Morrie and Mrs. Frank?" I said.

"Long enough," my mother said, shrugging.

"Why didn't you say something?" I said.

"To whom, darling?" she said. "Who should I have told?"

I paused to think about it. It was a very good question.

147

"Well, I guess Mr. Frank for starters," I said. "He's been a friend of yours even before I was born."

"So has Shirley, darling."

"But… what about? Geez, Mom. What… never mind," I said, shaking my head.

"It's not so easy, huh?" my mother said. "Shirley came to me because she didn't have anyone else she could talk about it with."

"Is it serious?" I said, still having a very hard time processing the information.

"Yes, darling," she said, sipping her coffee. "The Franks are talking divorce, and if they do get one, they'll probably be selling the grocery store. That is unless Jackson decides to resign as police chief and take it over."

"Jackson doesn't want to do that," I said.

"No, he doesn't," my mother said. "But the thought of the store being sold to someone outside the family bothers them a lot."

"And Morrie was the one who told Jackson?" Josie said.

"No, as soon as Shirley heard that Morrie was being questioned at the police station, she stopped by and told Jackson herself," my mother said. "The last thing she wanted was for Jackson to hear it from Morrie. And she was just worn out from keeping it a secret."

"Poor, Mr. Frank," I said.

"Yes, it's a very sad situation all around," my mother said.

148

She poured refills from the thermos, then leaned back in her seat and draped a leg over her knee.

"Is Howard going to be okay?" I said, desperate for a change of subjects.

"Yes, they think so," my mother said. "He appears to be in shock, and they're still worried about a concussion, but, overall, the doctor expects him to make a full recovery."

"He was lucky," I said.

"Certainly a lot luckier than Fatal Franny," Josie said.

"I wonder if Howard can identify the shooter," I said.

"The shooter? Really, darling," my mother said, shaking her head. "Why do you insist on watching so many police shows?"

"It relaxes me," I said, forcing a smile.

We stopped talking when we heard footsteps against the linoleum floor of the long hallway. I glanced up, expecting to see Jackson returning, but was surprised to see the widow Calducci and her bodyguard, Pee Wee, heading our way. Pee Wee held her by the elbow, but the widow seemed reasonably sober. Or she was simply well versed in walking while loaded.

"Good evening," the widow Calducci said, coming to a stop right next to us.

"Hello, Dot," my mother said.

"Have you heard how Howard is doing?" she said.

"Not really," my mother said, studying her closely. "But the doctor did say that he thinks he's going to be okay."

"That's wonderful," Dot said, sitting down in the vacant chair. "What a relief."

"Hi, Mrs. Calducci," I said. "Pee Wee."

They both managed a nod in my direction, and Pee Wee stood directly behind the widow and leaned against the wall.

"What a way to spend an evening," the widow Calducci said.

"Yes," I said. "If you don't mind my asking, how did you hear that Howard was in the hospital?"

Dot stared at me, then glanced over her shoulder at Pee Wee, who shrugged.

"I guess word just travels fast up here," Pee Wee said.

"Yes," Dot said. "Word travels fast."

Chapter 18

After receiving what the doctors told us would be the last update on Howard's condition until morning, we left the hospital just after three and went home. But after we made our morning rounds at the Inn, Josie and I headed back to the hospital to rejoin my mother outside Howard's room. A forlorn Jackson was already there waiting for his chance to speak with the mayor after he woke up and was cleared by the doctor.

When we arrived, Jackson managed a nod in our direction, but not much else. Josie and I hugged Jackson then sat down on either side of him. Even the coffee and breakfast sandwich Chef Claire had made for everyone barely cheered him up. And he stared off into space chewing and sipping coffee as a pile of biscuit crumbs began to form next to his chair.

"This is wonderful, darling," my mother said, slowly working her way through her sandwich.

For the record, it was a freshly-baked rosemary biscuit slathered with apple butter and wrapped around a poached egg and a slice of ham. Josie and I had polished off our first one before we got out of the kitchen.

"Chef Claire said she was sorry that she didn't have time to do a bit more with them," I said, still shaking my head at the fact that Chef Claire had insisted on making them.

"We told her she didn't have to do anything," Josie said, making short work of her second sandwich. "But we couldn't stop her."

"Never let her go," my mother said, chuckling softly.

"Good luck with that," Jackson said, still staring off into the distance.

I studied Jackson and couldn't decide if he was referring to his parents' problems or his own ongoing troubles with Chef Claire. Since it was probably a lot of both, I remained silent. A doctor came out of Howard's room and smiled at us.

"Hi, Doctor Wilbur," I said. "How he's doing?"

"Good morning, everyone," he said, smiling at us. "He's a lot better. He's still a bit unsure about some of the details, but certainly good enough to handle a few questions. But please keep it short, Jackson."

"What's that?" Jackson said, momentarily snapping out of his funk. "Oh, sure, Doc. Will do."

The doctor headed off down the hall, and Jackson got to his feet. I also stood and nodded at Josie and my mother. Jackson noticed.

"Where do you think you're going?" Jackson said.

"To see our good friend," I said, ignoring the real meaning behind his question. "Where else would we be going?"

"To snoop," Jackson said. "I think I should handle this by myself."

"Okay, Jackson," I said. "But I would have thought you'd want to keep a close eye on us while we're talking to Howard."

Jackson paused at the door. Then he nodded.

"Yeah, you're right," he said. "You're going to find your way into his room anyway. I might as well be around when you do."

"Thanks, Jackson," I said, beaming at him.

"Besides, given the mood I'm in," Jackson said. "I'm probably going to need all the help I can get."

All four of us entered the room and found Howard propped up in bed. He looked up from the magazine he was reading and gave us a small wave.

"Hey, guys," Howard said. "Thanks for stopping by."

"We were worried," my mother said. "How are you feeling?"

"Well, between the beating and the drugs they're giving me for the pain, I'm a little fuzzy."

"That's completely understandable, Howard," my mother said, patting his hand.

"Look, Howard, Doc Wilbur wants me to keep this short," Jackson said. "But if you're up for it, would you mind answering a few questions?"

"Of course not, Jackson," Howard said, setting the magazine aside and pressing a button that inclined the bed even more. "Whenever you're ready."

"What time did you and Franny leave to go out in your boat?" Jackson said.

"It was around two," Howard said.

"And where did you go?" Jackson said.

"It was your basic local tour," Howard said. "She'd never spent much time on the River, so I hit some of the high points. Then we headed for Lover's Cove around three, maybe half past."

"Why Lover's Cove?" Jackson said.

"Really, Jackson?" Howard said, laughing despite his obvious pain. "Certainly by now, you know that most of the boat rides I give women tend to include a stop at Lover's Cove. At least if I have anything to say about it."

"I just needed to ask, Howard," Jackson said. "So, your plans included a romantic component?"

"Romantic component?" I said, unable to contain myself.

"Don't start," Jackson said, glaring at me. "You'll get your chance."

"Yes, Jackson," Howard said. "I certainly had hopes that the afternoon would include a *romantic component*."

"So, you're at Lover's Cove with Franny and then what happened?" Jackson said.

"We were sitting on the boat next to each other looking at the shore with our backs to the water," Howard said. "And we were laughing and just starting to get friendly when two guys in masks climbed aboard my boat."

"You never saw their boat coming?" Jackson said.

"No, they must have paddled in the last hundred feet or so," Howard said. "And I was focused on other things at that moment and wasn't paying attention."

"And they were carrying guns?" Jackson said.

"Yes," Howard said, nodding. "And they caught us completely by surprise and quickly disarmed Franny. Then they tied her hands, tossed her into their boat which was right alongside mine, and then one of them started beating me."

I winced at the thought and studied the bruises on Howard's face.

"You poor man," my mother said.

"Thanks. I appreciate that," Howard said, smiling at my mother.

"Then what happened?" Jackson said.

"Well, when one of the guys was trying to wrestle Franny into their boat, she started kicking and fighting back the best she could. And the guy who was punching me landed a big one and knocked me backward. The boat was really rocking, and I ended up going over the side and landing in the water. That was when I decided I needed to get to shore. As you know, the water's pretty shallow over there so I started running the best I could through the water. The guy who'd been hitting me started shooting. But it took him a while to grab his gun, and the boat must have still been rocking back and forth because the shots were all over the place."

"How many shots did you hear?" Jackson said, jotting notes in his notebook.

"Let's see," Howard said, concentrating on the memory. "At least five, maybe more." Then he choked up and cleared his throat. "And then I heard the other shot a few minutes later after I managed to reach shore."

"The shot that killed Franny?" Jackson whispered.

"Yes," Howard said. "By then, I was hiding in the pines. But I did see one of the men shoot her at close range."

"And she was on the other boat when they shot her?" Jackson said.

"Yes."

"And then what happened?" Jackson said.

"I figured I was next on their list and did my best to hightail it out of there," Howard said. "I managed to work my way through the trees into the thick scrub, and then I hid out until it got dark. I was scared to death and pretty much out of it. At one point, I think I even passed out."

"Yes, I can see why," Jackson said, nodding. "Did they follow you?"

"They tried," Howard said. "But they gave up pretty quickly after they hit that scrub. It's a hard slog getting through that stuff, and I imagine they decided they needed to deal with Franny's body before another boat showed up. I was lucky I made it to shore where I did."

"And since they knew who you were, they probably thought they'd just track you down and finish things up at another time," I said.

"Darling!" my mother said.

"Now there's a cheery thought," Josie said, shaking her head at me.

"What?" I said. "I'm just pointing out a simple fact. I'm sure Howard has already considered that possibility. Right, Howard?"

"Well, actually, Suzy," he said, frowning. "Up until now, I really haven't had the chance to think about that. But I'm sure I will be now."

"Sorry, Howard," I mumbled.

"Did you get a good look at the two guys?" Jackson said.

"Not their faces," Howard said. "They never took their masks off. But one of them was huge."

"Pee Wee huge?" I said, trying to recover.

"Yeah," Howard said, staring off into space and nodding. "Definitely. The other guy who beat me up was smaller but really strong."

"Lean and well-muscled?" I said.

"Now that you mention it, yeah," Howard said. "He was definitely athletic. He was sort of built like a running back."

"Or a boxer?" I said, glancing at Josie.

"Yeah, maybe," Howard said. "That makes sense. Especially given the way he beat the crap out of me. He seemed to know what he was doing."

Howard yawned and pointed at the glass of water sitting on a nearby table. My mother held the glass for him while he drank from a straw.

"Thanks," Howard said, smiling at my mother. "Are you almost done, Jackson? I'm starting to fade a bit here."

"Sure. Just a couple more questions for now," Jackson said, glancing at me.

"Howard," I said. "We were in Lover's Cove just after all this happened."

"You were?" he said, frowning.

"Yes, Josie and I took the dogs for a swim, and we saw your boat there," I said. "And we went looking for you and Franny."

"You did?" Howard said, squinting up at me. "On shore?"

"Yes. And we spent about twenty minutes trying to find you," I said. "Didn't you hear us calling your name?"

"I think I remember hearing voices," Howard said. "But I was in pretty much out of it, and I just assumed it was the people who attacked us." He shook his head. "Boy, if you guys had managed to find me, that would have changed things, huh?"

"How did you end up on the side of the road?" I said.

"After it got dark, I started to work my way through the woods until I found the trail that leads up to the road. You know the one that runs through the back of Wellesley Island?"

"I do. And you managed to make it all that way?" I said, impressed. "That must have been three or four miles."

"It certainly seemed like it," Howard said. "I don't know how I kept going. But I knew that if I didn't, it could be weeks before somebody found my body. I eventually made it to the road, and then I must have just passed out. The next thing I remember is waking up in this bed."

"Well, you're safe and sound now," my mother said, glaring at me.

"Let it go, Mom," I whispered, still chagrined by my earlier faux pas.

"I sure hope so," Howard said, yawning. "Say, have you had any luck yet figuring out who might have killed Calducci?"

"No, nothing yet," Jackson said. "But I think I have a couple people I need to talk to."

"You mean the two who attacked Franny and me?"

"Yeah," Jackson said. "I've already talked with Pee Wee, but it couldn't hurt to have another chat with him and see where he was yesterday afternoon. I'm not sure who the other guy is, but maybe Pee Wee can shed some light on that."

"Uh, we might be able to help you out with that one, Jackson," I said.

"What? You know who he is?"

"Maybe," I said, glancing at Josie.

"It sounds like one of the guys who's been working on our renovation at the Inn," Josie said.

"That's interesting. And would you happen to know where this guy is at the moment?" Jackson said.

"Yeah," I said. "He's in our first-floor bathroom."

Chapter 19

If Rocco was surprised to see a cop standing behind him through the bathroom mirror, he didn't let on. Instead, he simply set the crowbar down, brushed as much plaster and dust off himself as he could, then washed his hands and face and followed Jackson into the kitchen where Josie and I were already waiting.

"I'm sorry to bother you, Rocco," Jackson said, sitting down next to me at the island. "It is Rocco, right?"

"Yes, Rocco's fine," he said, taking a seat and giving Jackson a blank stare. "How can I help you?"

"I'm just following up on a lead," Jackson said.

"I see," Rocco said, glancing at me.

Even though his glance was gentle and didn't linger, it still made the hairs on the back of my neck tingle.

"Yesterday afternoon our mayor was attacked by two men when he was out on the River," Jackson said. "One of the men fits your description."

"Does he now?" Rocco said, reaching for one of the cookies we'd set on the table. He took a bite and nodded. "These are good. Hazelnuts? No, almond."

"Macadamia," Josie said, reaching for her third.

"Really? I'm picking up a hint of almond," Rocco said, examining his cookie.

"Chef Claire uses just a touch of Amaretto," Josie said.

"Smart," Rocco said, nodding and completely ignoring the stare Jackson was giving him.

"Now that we have the mystery of the cookie solved, I was wondering if you'd mind telling me where you were yesterday afternoon," Jackson said.

"I was out of town," Rocco said, casually reaching for the last cookie.

"Were you by yourself?" Jackson said.

"No, I was with Pee Wee," Rocco said. "You know Pee Wee? Big guy, no neck. He works for Mrs. Calducci."

Rocco's response caught me by surprise, and I paused mid-bite. It was almost enough to make me put my cookie down, but Josie, already on the prowl for more, was sitting too close for comfort.

"Yes, I'm familiar with him," Jackson said.

"Pee Wee is hard to miss," Rocco said.

"Can I ask what the two of you were doing?" Jackson said.

"We were doing some shopping across the River in Kingston," Rocco said.

"In the afternoon?" Jackson said.

"Yes."

"And you went by boat," Jackson said.

"Yes."

"Whose boat was it?"

"Pee Wee said it was one of Calducci's," Rocco said.

"What kind of boat was it?" Jackson said.

"I don't know," Rocco said, shrugging. "I'm not much of a boat guy. As long as the thing floats and moves in the right direction, I'm happy. But if you have a description of the guys who attacked your mayor, then you must also have a description of the boat."

"So?" Jackson said.

"So, if you already have it, why are you bothering me about it?" Rocco said.

I watched their exchange closely. As much experience Jackson had at asking questions, Rocco appeared even better at answering them. Rocco sat quietly waiting for Jackson's response, and I couldn't shake the feeling that Rocco was definitely telling the truth.

"I'm merely trying to establish your whereabouts yesterday afternoon, Rocco," Jackson said.

"I just told you. I was shopping in Kingston with Pee Wee," Rocco said.

"And I'm sure that Canadian Immigration will confirm that?" Jackson said.

"What?" Rocco said, confused.

"Did you check in with Canadian Immigration when you landed?" Jackson said.

"Why on earth would we do that?" Rocco said.

"Because it's the law," Jackson said.

"Really? Huh. I did not know that," Rocco said, then smiled at Jackson. "Well done, Chief. You caught me. Do I pay a fine, or do you just want the rest of my cookie?"

Josie and I smiled at each other. Jackson did his best to ignore Rocco's comment.

"How about credit card receipts?" Jackson said. "If you went shopping, there must be a record of what you bought."

"I always pay cash," Rocco said. "Over the years, I've found that the more electronic trails I leave, the more people like you want to talk to me."

"Yeah, it's funny how that works, Rocco," Jackson said, flipping through his notepad. "Do you know where Pee Wee is at the moment?"

"No," Rocco said. "I haven't seen him since he dropped me off at the town dock yesterday."

"What time was that?" Jackson said.

"Around seven. Then I headed straight to the Water's Edge for a burger and a couple of beers."

"Good call," Josie said, then paused when she caught the look Jackson was giving her. She shrugged and gave him a small smile. "They have great burgers."

Rocco laughed and gave Josie the last half of his cookie.

"You're too much," Rocco said to Josie as he got up from his stool. "You got anything else for me, Chief? I promised these ladies that I'd finish up this week, and I'm falling behind schedule."

"Just one more thing," Jackson said.

"Yes?"

"Howard said that the man who fits your description beat him up pretty badly," Jackson said.

Rocco didn't wait for Jackson to ask the question. He placed both his hands down on the kitchen island and spread his fingers wide.

"You must have some experience with fights, Chief," Rocco said, staring down at his hands.

"Sure. I've been around my share," Jackson said.

"Then I'm sure you know the damage that a fight does to someone's hands whether they win or lose. Do these hands look like they've recently been in a fight?"

I glanced down at Rocco's hands. They didn't. In fact, they looked they'd been recently manicured. And they looked a lot better than my nails did at the moment.

"No, they don't," Jackson said. "But you could have been wearing gloves."

"Yeah, I could," Rocco said. "Did your mayor happen to mention that the guy was wearing gloves?"

"Actually, no, he didn't," Jackson said.

"That's kind of a hard detail to miss wouldn't you say, Chief?" Rocco said. "As I'm sure you know, if I hit you with a fist, you'd know if I was wearing a glove straight away. Not only does it look different, it feels different."

"Yes," Jackson said, conceding the point. "It does."

"I'm going to get back to work," Rocco said. "Thanks for the cookies, ladies. Please pass along my compliments to Chef Claire."

"The guy has to be involved," Jackson said after Rocco had left the kitchen.

"Maybe," I said.

"C'mon, Suzy," Jackson said. "What are the odds that it was two different guys who match Howard's description?"

"They're pretty low," I said. "But maybe it was another guy instead of Rocco who was with Pee Wee."

"I guess it's possible," Jackson said. "The lack of bruises on his hands is a problem."

"For you," Josie said. "Not for Rocco. I'd say that might just clear him."

"What now?" I said.

"I need to track Pee Wee down and have another chat with him," Jackson said.

"Have the state police had any luck?" I said.

"No, I spoke with Detective Abrams this morning. And they aren't getting anywhere with Calducci's murder. But they are leaning toward Pee Wee for the attack on Howard."

"Howard's word against the word of two known criminals might be enough, right?" Josie said.

"It might," Jackson said. "But the fact they were wearing masks complicates things. And the description of the clothing

Howard gave me doesn't match what Rocco was wearing at the Water's Edge last night."

"It's not that hard to pull off a change of clothes," Josie said.

"No," Jackson said. "But the lack of bruises is potentially a show-stopper. At least as far as Rocco is concerned. You heard Howard's description of the beating he got. It was brutal."

"Well, if Rocco wasn't involved, who was the other guy?" I said.

"I'm sure Pee Wee has dozens of people he could have used," Jackson said.

"Maybe we should try to talk with the four guys who came in for lunch the day of the funeral," I said. "Since they've been identified as four of Calducci's lieutenants, then… why are you staring at me?"

"We?" Jackson said, raising an eyebrow.

"I was referring to the collective *we*, Jackson," I said.

Josie snorted. I ignored the looks I was getting from both of them.

"Let's change the subject, shall *we*?" Josie said, rummaging through the fridge. "Have you decided what you're getting Chef Claire for her birthday?"

"I have," Jackson said, his mood brightening. "I decided to go all out."

"And just roll the dice to see if you can force her hand?" Josie said, grinning at me.

"Actually, yes," Jackson said. "How did you know that?"

"Just a lucky guess," Josie said.

"And would your gift just happen to go well with the diamond tennis bracelet you got her for Christmas?" I said.

Jackson thought about it for a few seconds then nodded.

"As a matter of fact, they'd look great together," Jackson said.

"This is bad," Josie whispered.

"Yeah, this can't end well," I whispered back.

"What are you two babbling about?" Jackson said.

"Nothing," I said. "Just a little girl talk."

Chapter 20

We walked the perimeter of our property marveling at the job the work crew had done with our renovation. Inside, the workers were finishing the painting, and several boxes of new dog beds, toys, and snacks had been delivered and were ready to go. We'd been working with various shelters in the area that didn't have the no-kill policy we did, and we were about to add thirty-two new dogs to our rescue population. The dogs would start arriving over the next few weeks, and we could finally stop worrying about being ready to have room for them.

"We're about to become Dog Rescue Central," Josie said, laughing.

"That was our plan all along, right?" I said. "And we need to get rolling on hiring some new staff."

"Yeah, we do," Josie said. "I'm just excited that it's actually happening. We're kind of like a sanctuary city for dogs."

"I like that," I said, nodding. "Oh, there's Sammy. Are you ready?"

"Let's do it," Josie said, walking across the lawn. "Okay, Sammy. Go ahead and put him down. Let's see how he does."

Sammy gently placed Oslo on the ground and removed the leash attached to the dog's collar. Josie sat down on the grass and clapped her hands together.

"Come here, Oslo. Good boy."

I watched Oslo take his first few tentative steps. It was the first time he'd been outside without a leash since Josie had performed the brain surgery. Oslo found his footing, got some confidence, then trotted toward Josie. When he reached her, he rolled over on his back and waited for a tummy rub. Then Josie rolled a tennis ball about ten feet away and watched Oslo retrieve it and drop it at her feet.

"Look at him," I said, tearing up. "He's going to make it, isn't he?"

"I think so. The biopsy came back clean," Josie said, wiping her eyes with the back of her hand. "Sammy, could you go get Tripod? I'd like to see how Oslo handles being around another dog off the leash."

Sammy headed inside the Inn and soon returned with Tripod, his three-legged cocker spaniel we'd rescued from an illegal puppy mill operating in the area several months ago. The dog had lost its leg due to frostbite, but was fully recovered and had adapted to the point where it was easy to forget he only had three legs. I watched the dogs, both saved by Josie's magic hands, gently roughhouse with each other and roll around on the grass.

"You did great," I said.

"Thanks," Josie said.

"Do you ever think what your life would be like if you weren't doing this?" I said, leaning back in the grass and letting the warm sun wash over me.

"I do my best not to," Josie said, laughing. "That would be a nightmare. Sammy, I think that's enough for today. Take Oslo back inside and get him settled in. Then start checking his vitals on the hour the rest of the day. I want to make sure he doesn't have any setbacks."

"You got it," Sammy said, picking Oslo up and heading back inside with Tripod following close behind.

"I suppose we're going to need to start looking for a good home for Oslo," I said.

"Well, Morrie the Meat Guy did offer to take him," Josie said.

"That was before we found out he was sleeping with Jackson's mom," I said. "We can't reward that sort of behavior."

"Am I hearing a touch of sanctimony?" Josie said, climbing to her feet and brushing herself off.

"Yeah, maybe a bit," I said. "I'm sure it wouldn't have any impact on how Morrie would treat Oslo, but the idea bothers me."

"What Morrie and Mrs. Frank do isn't any of our business, Suzy," Josie said.

"I know. But what if Morrie is somehow involved in Calducci's murder?"

"Highly unlikely," Josie said, walking toward the Inn. "And you know it."

"You're not being very helpful," I said.

"Disagree."

171

I gently punched her arm as we strolled back inside.

"Freddie called earlier about meeting after work for a drink," I said.

"That sounds great," Josie said. "You can grill him about Calducci why I focus on what he got Chef Claire for her birthday."

"You don't think it's possible that they both decided to spring an engagement ring on her, do you?" I said.

"Unfortunately, I do," Josie said. "That's exactly the sort of thing those two would do."

"Yeah. And they did manage to buy her the identical bracelet last Christmas," I said. "Can you imagine the spot that would put Chef Claire in?"

"Yes, I can," Josie said. "And that's exactly why we need to make sure the two of them don't do anything that stupid."

"Good luck trying to talk either one of them out of it," I said. "You know what it's like when they have their minds made up about something."

Josie gave me a sideways glance and smiled.

"Yeah, I think I could ballpark it," she said.

"My *focus*, for lack of a better term, is completely different from how Jackson and Freddie approach problems and you know it," I said.

"Suzy, at the risk of repeating myself, disagree."

Chapter 21

We left the house early to stop for gas on our way to the restaurant. I pulled up to one of the pumps and waved to Charlie, the owner, who was inside the convenience store and staring out through the large picture window. Adjacent to the gas pumps was Howard's parking lot that extended off the back of his pharmacy. I was surprised to see his car parked outside the rear entrance.

I tapped on the passenger seat window, and Josie lowered the window.

"Check the oil, please," she deadpanned. "And I think the front left tire might need some air."

"Funny," I said, nodding at Howard's car. "Do you think Howard's back at work already?"

"I'd be surprised," Josie said. "Maybe he just stopped by to check in on how things are going. Or maybe to fill his prescriptions."

"I wonder if he's remembered anything else about the other day," I said.

"And you think we should just pop in and say hi?" Josie said.

"It couldn't hurt, right?" I said.

"How about we let the guy recover before we start pestering him with a bunch of questions?" Josie said.

"I'm not going to pester him. Plus, it would be rude for us not check in and make sure he's okay," I said. "And we wouldn't want to be rude."

"No, of course not," Josie said. "You'd hate to be rude. Just incredibly nosy."

When the tank was full, I hopped back in the SUV, drove away from the pumps, and parked next to Howard's car, covering a distance of about forty feet. We entered the pharmacy through the back door and found Howard taking inventory.

"Hi, folks," he said, silently counting to himself. "Can I help you find something or did you just stop by to say hello?"

"We saw your car and just thought we'd check in and see how you're doing," I said. "Isn't it a bit early for you to be back at work?"

"Thanks for thinking of me. I appreciate it. The doc said I could do a couple of hours a day as long as I took it easy," Howard said. "But between you and me, I think I should probably be home in bed."

"Then go home and go to bed, Howard," I said.

"I will," he said, silently counting items on another shelf.

I glanced around and noticed the boarded up window.

"Is that where the robbers came in?" I said.

"Yup. I was going to get it fixed the other day," Howard said, forcing a small smile. "But something came up."

"You mean like getting the stuffing beaten out of you?" Josie said.

174

"Yeah, it's always something, right?" he said, chuckling.

"Well, at least you haven't lost your sense of humor," Josie said.

"Do you think the two incidents are connected, Howard?" I said.

"The burglary and the attack on the boat?" Howard said, frowning as he sat down on top of a stack of boxes.

"Yeah."

"Well, I guess they have to be, right?" he said. "I'm pretty sure that everything that's happened the past week is all connected with the future of Calducci's operation. And with who's going to control it."

"What about Dot?" I said.

"What about her?" Howard said.

"What do you think is going to happen to her?" I said.

"Who knows?" Howard said, shrugging. "Dot has two basic choices. She can either get herself cleaned up or continue destroying herself until her brain looks like something you'd find in the produce section."

I flinched when I heard the blunt, graphic metaphor he used. But I couldn't argue with its validity.

"My Mom mentioned what happened with you and Dot. About how she broke things off with you and took up with Calducci," I said. "I'm sorry."

"Hey, don't worry about it," Howard said, shrugging. "Ancient history. But still, she felt the need to send her goons after me. Go figure."

"You mean Pee Wee?" I said.

"Yeah, who else could it have been?" Howard said.

"Why would she want to hurt you, Howard?"

"That's the million dollar question that's been rolling around my head," Howard said. "I'm hoping that it was Franny she wanted to take out, and I just got caught up in the crossfire."

He sounded both sad and bitter, and it was obvious that his relationship with Dot was a very old wound that had recently been reopened and was bleeding fresh.

"When was the last time you saw Jimmy Calducci?" I said.

"You mean before I saw him at dinner the night you opened the restaurant?" Howard said.

"Yeah."

"Gee, I'll have to think about that," Howard said. "I know it was several years ago. Jimmy rarely made it up here."

"I heard he was thinking about buying a summer place on the River," I said.

"Really?" Howard said. "I didn't know that. But Jimmy and I never made much of an effort to stay in touch."

"Do you know anything about the inner workings of Calducci's operation?" I said.

"Not a thing," Howard said. "Why do you ask?"

"Well, like you, I can't come up with any other reason why all these things are happening. It has to be about people fighting for control of Calducci's operation." I said.

"Yeah, that's the only thing that makes sense," Howard said. "And it has to be connected with the robbery here. Calducci overdosing on painkillers and booze should have been a perfect way to take him out and not raise suspicions. You know, make his death look accidental, maybe even suicide."

"From what we heard from Freddie," I said. "They did a pretty good job of hiding their tracks."

"I imagine they've had lots of practice," Howard said. "But all that matters is that they were successful, and the planet's in better shape because of it."

"That's pretty harsh, Howard," I said.

"Yeah, I guess it is," Howard said, giving me a hard stare. "But I was recently beaten within an inch of my life by two of Calducci's goons, so you'll have to excuse my lack of sympathy for the deceased."

"I didn't mean to upset you, Howard," I said.

"Forget it," he said. "It's probably just me overreacting. I'm kind of a mess these days."

"That's completely understandable, Howard," Josie said, giving me the *wrap it up* look.

"Did Franny say anything on the boat?" I said.

"What do you mean?" Howard said, standing up to resume his inventory count.

"Did she say something that might be useful for figuring this all out?" I said. "Did Franny say anything about why she was still hanging around town?"

"Yeah, she did, actually," Howard said, sitting back down on the stack of boxes. "Whew, I'm beat."

"Then go home," Josie said, shooting me a dirty look. "All of this can wait."

"I will," he said. "Franny said she was still here looking for Calducci's killer. You remember the promise she made at the funeral."

"Did she happen to mention if she'd made any progress?" I said.

Howard removed a bottle of pills from his white coat and swallowed two with a long swig of water.

"She was about to," Howard said, his voice barely above a whisper. "She said she had figured it out and was about to do something about it."

"Really?" I said, feeling the hairs on the back of my neck tingle. "What happened then?"

"Those two guys showed up," Howard said, exhaling loudly. "Then all hell broke loose, and she never got the chance to tell me."

"Did you tell this to Jackson?" I said.

"Sure. And the state cops," he said, shrugging. "But without some real evidence, what good is it going to do?"

"But you're sure Pee Wee was one of the men?" I said.

"I'm positive," Howard said. "Who else could it have been?"

"But he has an alibi that he was in Kingston shopping all afternoon," I said.

"Yeah, Jackson told me," he said. "I guess criminals are good at covering their tracks."

"How long were the two guys there with you and Franny?" I said.

"Uh, Suzy, no offense," Howard said, his voice measured. "But I've already been through this several times with the people who are actually responsible for figuring all this out. And you know that I love you to death, but you're giving me a headache."

Before I could respond, Josie grabbed my arm and gently pulled me toward the door.

"We're sorry to bother you, Howard," Josie said. "Inspector Clouseau here just can't control herself at times."

"Funny," I said.

But inside I felt terrible about upsetting our friend and adding to his misery. To his credit, Howard forced a laugh and waved it off.

"Don't worry about it," he said.

"We're heading to C's for dinner," Josie said. "Since you won't go home and go to bed, if you're up for it, you're welcome to join us."

"Thanks, Josie. But I think I will go home. It appears I overdid it today."

179

Josie waved goodbye and nudged me toward the exit.

"I'm sorry, Howard," I managed on my way out the door. Chagrined, I climbed in the driver's seat and started the car. "Not one of my finer moments."

"Probably not," Josie said. "But your intentions were good."

"It's like there's a switch that goes on and I can never seem to turn it off," I said. "I feel terrible."

"Maybe dinner will help," Josie said, fastening her seat belt. "I'm starving."

"What on earth is the matter with me?" I said.

"Well, for one, at the moment you've got the car in park," she said. "Let's go."

"No, I'm serious," I said. "There must be something seriously wrong with me."

Josie sat back in her seat and glanced over at me. She placed a hand on my knee and spoke in a hushed tone.

"Suzy, we've been through this many times in the past, and I'm sure we'll go through it again. So I'm going to tell you the same thing I always do when we find ourselves in this situation."

"Yes?"

"Shut up and drive."

It wasn't much of a drive, and I managed to navigate the block and a half without inflicting any more self-abuse. We headed inside C's, waved to several friends, and made our way to the kitchen to say hello to Chef Claire. It was early, but she was already buried behind a long row of order slips, so we kept it brief and headed for my mother's table.

"Is your mom coming?" Josie said, scanning the menu.

"No, it's Montreal day," I said, glancing around the crowded dining room.

Once a month, my mother spent the day in Montreal shopping, eating, shopping, eating, going to the theater, and, if there was still time, some more shopping before heading back to her hotel.

"Do you think I should apologize to Howard again?" I said.

"Just try to forget it, Suzy," Josie said. "If you try apologizing, you'll probably end up asking him a whole bunch of new questions."

"Yeah, you're probably right," I said, focusing on the four men who were having an animated conversation with our hostess. "What's going on over there?"

Josie glanced over her shoulder and watched the conversation that looked like it was about to get heated.

"Aren't those the four guys that were here for lunch the day of Calducci's funeral?" she said.

"I think so," I said, continuing to watch our hostess trying to explain herself to the four men. "They were his lieutenants, right? It looks like they might be giving Wendy a hard time. I'll be right back."

I got up from the table and approached the group. Wendy looked relieved to see me.

"Hi, Wendy," I said, smiling and glancing around at the men. "Is there a problem?"

"Yeah, there's a problem," one of the men said, glaring at Wendy. "Somebody lost our reservation."

"Sir, please accept my sincerest apologies," Wendy said, obviously shaken. "I don't know how this could have happened. We've never had a problem with our system losing a reservation." She looked over at me. "Suzy, I'm so sorry about this."

"Don't worry about it, Wendy. We'll figure it out."

The man moved his glare from Wendy to me. Over the years, I've learned that most stares are easy to return or even avoid. Others immediately got your attention. But it is the rare pair of eyes that can reach inside and squeeze your stomach and make the hairs on the back of your neck stand up. This glare was so good that I found myself wondering if he'd learned it from my mother.

I forced myself to take a deep breath. If the guy reacted this way to a botched dinner reservation, I wouldn't want to be around when he actually had a real reason to get mad.

"And you are?" the man eventually said.

"Going to fix your problem, sir," I said, giving him the best smile I could summon.

"That would be nice. How hard can it be to get a dinner reservation right?"

"How about we avoid the rhetorical for the moment and just focus on getting this problem resolved?"

The man's glare softened a bit, and a hint of a smile appeared and then vanished. Before I could bask in my minor victory, I noticed one of the other men nervously shifting back and forth on his feet. But I ignored him and refocused on the man with the angry stare.

"Just give us a minute, sir," I said, then turned to Wendy. "What else do we have available?"

"That's the problem, Suzy. We're booked solid until nine."

"That's way too late," the man said. "We made the reservation for seven."

The man who was shifting back and forth shifted into overdrive, and it was my turn to stare. He was looking down at the floor and unable to make eye contact with anyone. Eventually, I couldn't watch his nervous shuffle any longer.

"Sir, if you need to pee, the men's bathroom is right over there," I said, pointing.

"No, I'm fine," the man whispered.

"Then what on earth is the matter with you, Paulie?" the angry man said. "You're hopping around like hot grease on a griddle."

"It's nothing, Lou," Paulie said, glancing up.

At least he'd stopped shuffling for the moment.

"What is wrong with you?" Lou said, then waited for an answer.

Paulie's shoulders drooped, and he eventually gave Lou a small shrug.

"I forgot to make the reservation."

"What?" Lou said.

"Yeah, I got busy and forgot to do it," Paulie said. "I didn't think it was going to be a problem."

"You let me stand here and berate these fine women?"

"Yeah."

"And you thought you'd just stand by and let me make a complete fool of myself?"

"I didn't mean to do that, Lou," Paulie said. "And the situation escalated so quickly."

I watched the exchange play out. If Paulie hadn't needed to pee before, I was pretty sure he did now. Lou stared at Paulie, then nodded and turned to Wendy and me.

"Ladies, I owe you a sincere apology. As you can see, sometimes I'm forced to travel in the company of less than honorable men."

"Don't worry about it," I said. "Things happen."

"Not to me they don't," Lou said. "Now, if you'll excuse us, we'll be on our way. Again, I'm very sorry for the way I acted."

He wheeled around and headed for the door, closely followed by the other three men. I watched them leave, then my snoop switch turned itself on.

"No, wait," I said, calling after them. I turned to Wendy. "Josie and I are at my mother's table, and it's just the two of us.

And we haven't even ordered yet. Please have our table set for six." I turned back to Lou. "I'd be honored if you'd join us for dinner."

Lou transitioned into the perfect gentleman, and he beamed at me. To be honest, the ease at which he completed the transformation caught me by surprise and made me nervous.

"You see that, Paulie?" Lou said. "That's how people of honor conduct themselves. You could learn a lot from this woman." Then he looked at me. "I'm sorry. I didn't catch your name."

"I'm Suzy. Suzy Chandler."

"Suzy Chandler," Lou said, extending his hand. "I know your mother. And she's told me many wonderful things about you."

"I wouldn't put too much stock in what she says. She's a drinker."

I returned the handshake as Lou laughed and squeezed my hand. I gestured for the four men to follow me and led them to our table where Josie was trying to drown a piece of Italian bread in olive oil. She looked up surprised and with a mouthful of bread.

"These gentlemen will be joining us for dinner," I said.

"They will?"

"Yes. They had a problem with their reservation."

"I see," Josie said, glancing around at all four men with a genuine smile. "That's great. Good evening, gentlemen."

It was obvious this was the first time the men had gotten a good look at Josie. And their reactions were predictable. They gushed hellos and did their best not to stare at her as they sat down. Most of them failed miserably. Only Lou, who I decided was their de-facto leader, managed to avoid overt leering.

"Gentlemen, this is Josie, my business partner."

I heard the words come out of my mouth and found the label I'd given her unsatisfactory. But telling them that Josie was my best friend in the whole world and someone I'd run through fire for was a bit too much of a mouthful, so I settled for business partner.

"You're the veterinarian," Lou said, obviously impressed. "The one who performed brain surgery on Jimmy's dog, right?"

"Guilty as charged," Josie said, reaching for another piece of bread.

"I'm Lou. How's the dog doing?"

"We think he's going to be okay," Josie said.

"That's great. He's a good dog," Lou said, forcing his eyes off Josie and onto his menu. Then he put the menu down. "I'm sorry. That was rude of me. I forgot the rest of the introductions. "This is Paulie, and he's the reason we're sitting here with you at the moment. So I guess I should say thank you, Paulie."

"You're welcome," Paulie said, not looking up from his menu.

"You think you might be able to do a little surgery on his brain?" Lou said, nodding at Paulie. "He could use a tune up."

"Sure," Josie deadpanned as she gave Paulie's head the quick once over. "Bring him by tomorrow morning around nine."

Lou laughed. Paulie didn't find it quite as funny and only managed a fake smile.

"Relax, Paulie. I'm just having a little fun with you," Lou said. "Next to him is Francis,"

"Hi, Francis," I said, glancing at the large man with tiny eyes that, at first glance, appeared to be closed.

"Francis," Josie said. "Like the Pope."

"Yeah," Francis said, nodding. "It's my new nickname and sort of an inside joke."

"Really?" I said, waiting for the punchline.

"You know, just like the Pope," Lou said. "When you see him, the first thing you do is start praying."

Lou started laughing, and the other three men joined in. Their laughter could have been genuine, but I was left with the feeling that laughing at Lou's jokes was part of the job description.

"And on my right is Whispers," Lou said.

"It's nice to meet you, Whispers," I said, smiling at the small man whose eyes kept darting around the restaurant but never seemed to land on anything specific.

Whispers responded quietly, and I had absolutely no idea what he said. I glanced at Josie.

"I got nothing," Josie whispered.

187

Lou chuckled and placed an arm on Whispers' shoulder.

"He's aptly named, to say the least," Lou said. "Isn't that right, Whispers?"

Again, Whispers said something that sounded like a quick burst of wind. Lou listened carefully, then gave up and sat back in his seat.

"Yeah, whatever," Lou said, refocusing on his menu. "By the way, dinner is on me."

Our waitress approached, waved to Josie and me, and took our orders. She answered all the men's questions, which were numerous, and suggested wine pairings where appropriate. She even managed to get Whispers' order on the first take.

I had no idea how she managed to do that. To me, it sounded like Whispers had mumbled *pffffft* several times in a row.

"So, how long are you guys going to be in town, Lou?" I said, then flinched when Josie kicked my foot under the table.

"Just another day or two. But the weather has been so good we decided to take some time off and enjoy the River."

"That's great," I said, beginning to frame my next question. I ignored the glare Josie was giving me. "It's really too bad about what happened to Mr. Calducci."

"Yeah," Lou said.

The other three men watched Lou's reaction and then nodded along sympathetically.

"And Franny," I said, letting it hang in the air.

Whispers was the first one to snort.

That I heard.

"Yeah, it's too bad about Franny," Lou said.

"Did you work with her?" I said.

"Nobody really worked with Franny," Lou said. "You kinda worked alongside her."

"Well, you sure didn't want to work *in front* of her," Francis deadpanned.

All four men burst out laughing. Josie and I watched it play out and waited until they finished.

Sorry about that, Franny. Whatever grieving process these men had gone through over your recent demise appeared to be over.

"Any ideas who might have wanted to kill her?" I said, going for casual but probably crossing the line into nosy.

The other three men fell silent and glanced at Lou, waiting to take their cue from his reaction. Lou took a sip of wine and wiped his mouth with his napkin.

"Suzy, that's a very long list of people. You'd save yourself a lot of time by looking at people who didn't."

He said it with a smile, but I could tell I'd touched a nerve. Josie caught it as well and nodded her head at the ladies room. She stood up, excused herself from the table, and waited for me to follow her. We entered and looked around to make sure we were the only ones there.

"An hour ago, you said you felt terrible about asking all those annoying questions," she said, washing her hands.

"I did. With Howard."

"Unbelievable. What is it with you? Dial it down and find your off-switch. You do know who these guys are, right?"

"When else will we have a chance like this?" I said casually as I examined my makeup in the mirror.

"A chance to do what? Get shot?"

"Don't be dramatic," I said, touching up my lipstick. "We're just having a quiet dinner."

"If you want a quiet dinner, then I suggest you let Whispers do all the talking," Josie said.

Unable to maintain her frustration with me, Josie cracked up. I laughed along.

"He is odd, isn't he?" I said.

"Just do me a favor. Keep the questions general and whatever you do, don't suggest that any of them could have been involved."

"Do you think they were?" I said, glancing at her through the mirror.

"Of course I do. That's why I'm telling you not to suggest it."

"Good point," I said, heading for the door.

We headed back to the table and discovered that our appetizers had arrived. All four men stood, then settled back in, and the six of us ate in silence.

"I like women who have a healthy appetite," Lou said, obviously impressed with our ability to match him bite for bite.

"Then you're going to love, Josie," I said.

"Funny," Josie said, reaching for another roasted red pepper.

"What did we miss?" I said to Lou.

"Not much. We were just sitting here wondering out loud who might have shot Fatal Franny."

I choked down the last of a slice of red pepper and took a sip of water.

"And what did you come up with?" I said, beaming at Lou.

"Just the usual suspects," Lou said, helping himself to a stuffed mushroom.

"What about Calducci?" I blurted.

My question was enough to force Josie to put her fork down.

"What about him?" Lou said, also placing his utensils on his plate.

"Uh, well, since you were talking about Franny, I just thought you could have also discussed who might have been involved in Mr. Calducci's death."

"Well, we weren't," Lou said.

"Sure, sure," I said, nodding. "I was wondering about something."

"You were, huh?" Lou said, studying me closely.

"Yes, I was wondering what impact Mr. Calducci's death would have on his overall business operations."

Lou picked up his knife and fork and shook his head as he resumed eating.

"I heard you were a tenacious little thing," he said, chuckling.

"Really? From who?" I said, glancing at Josie.

"Don't look at me," she said, reaching for the plate of stuffed mushrooms.

"You have a reputation for being a bit of a snoop," Lou said. "And it's obviously well-earned."

"I'm just curious by nature, that's all."

"Do yourself a favor, Suzy," Lou said. "Stay out of this one. Whoever did whatever they did to Jimmy Calducci had their reasons."

"Do you know what the reasons were?" I said, unable to stop myself.

Lou again set his knife and fork down and took a sip of wine. He wiped his mouth, then looked at me.

"Not that it's any of your business, no. I don't know what the reasons were. All I know is that it happened, and we're going to have to wait and see how things play out."

"Because there's a lot at stake for your various businesses, right?" I said, leaning forward and placing my elbows on the table.

Lou shook his head and glanced over at Josie.

"Isn't there something you can do to control her?"

"I was hoping to learn a few tricks from you, Lou," Josie deadpanned.

"Funny," I said, glaring at her.

Lou and the rest of the men did find it funny, and they laughed until our waitress arrived with our entrees. We sat quietly until she had served everyone and refilled our wine glasses. I took a bite of my steak, then started in again.

"I don't mean to be rude, but it would seem that the death of a man in Calducci's position would create havoc in his organization."

"Lou," Francis said, giving me the evil eye. "She's putting me off my food."

"It's okay, Francis," Lou said. "I'll handle this. Just eat." Then he focused on me. "What exactly can I say that will make you drop this particular subject?"

Whispers uttered something I didn't get. But Lou did, and a big grin formed on his face as he continued to stare at me.

"Yeah," Lou said, nodding. "You'd like that wouldn't you, Whispers?"

The hairs on the back of my neck stood straight up. I gulped and felt my hand tremble as I reached for my glass of water. I took a sip and made eye contact with Lou. It was obvious his question was a serious one, and I decided I couldn't back down now.

A note to all the amateur sleuths out there. Be careful what you wish for.

"Uh, okay. Let me see," I said. "I guess you could start by telling me if you think that Calducci's and Franny's deaths are connected."

"Yes, I do," Lou said, nodding.

"Do you think that the same person killed both of them?"

"Yes, probably."

"And do you think their deaths are linked to the issue of who's going to control Calducci's operation?"

"Maybe."

"Really?"

"What part of maybe don't you understand, Suzy?" Lou said, sipping wine.

"No, I got it," I said, frowning. "I was just expecting a different answer."

"Then aren't you glad you asked the question?" Lou said, chuckling.

Everyone at the table, except me, found his response funny, and I waited for the laughter to subside.

"Are you in line to take over Calducci's operation, Lou?" I said.

All four men flinched, and I saw Whispers shaking his head at me. But I managed to resume eye contact with Lou who was staring at me hard. I was surprised to see some admiration mixed in with his frustration and anger.

"I'll keep you posted," Lou said, softly. "Is there anything else?"

"Just one more question," I said.

"What's that?"

"How's your steak?"

Chapter 22

"Rocco, it looks fantastic."

I had to agree with Josie. The downstairs bathroom did look great, and apart from the smell of fresh paint, it was a showcase. I couldn't believe it was same space from a week ago.

"Thanks," Rocco said, rinsing his paint brush in the sink. "You sure you're happy with the color?"

"It's perfect," Josie said. "I've been thinking about painting my bedroom, and that color would look great in there, too. What's it called?"

"I think it's called Afternoon Magic or something like that. But I always refer to it as Mobster Sky Blue."

Over the past week, we'd discovered that Rocco loved to interject mobster references into his conversations whenever the opportunity presented itself. He thought he was funny and his patter was part of his boyish charm. Some of them were funny, most of them made us nervous, but they did serve as a helpful reminder about the background of the man who'd impressed us with his abilities wielding a crowbar and nail gun.

"Okay, Rocco," Josie said, nodding. "I'll play. Why is it called Mobster Sky Blue?"

"Because if you get whacked outside on a clear day, it's the last color you'll see," Rocco said. Then he glanced back and forth at us. "Get it?"

"Yeah, I got it," Josie said, frowning. "Good one. On second thought, maybe I'll just go with a yellow."

"How about some lunch?" I said.

"You read my mind."

"What do you say, Rocco?" I said. "The least we can do is feed you one last time."

"You talked me into it," Rocco said, setting the paintbrush aside to wash his hands. "You wouldn't happen to have any of that eggplant parmesan left, would you?"

Josie shook her head.

"Sorry, Rocco. You're a day late."

"Really?" he said, surprised. "That was a big tray."

"We needed to make room in the fridge for the ziti Chef Claire made," Josie said, shrugging.

"Yeah, that's the reason there's none left," I said.

We headed for the kitchen, and I poured iced tea for the three of us while Josie grabbed the tray of ziti from the fridge. She cut a huge chunk from it and put it in the microwave. While we waited, I wrote Rocco's final check and slid it across the island. He glanced at it, smiled, then slid it into his pocket.

"Be sure and let me know if you decide to do any more projects around the house," Rocco said.

"Will do, Rocco," I said. "You're really good."

"That was nothing," he said. "You should see me when I really get warmed up with that nail gun."

He gave me a mischievous grin.

197

"Rocco, I know you're joking," I said. "At least I hope you are. But sometimes the mobster references make me kinda nervous."

"Yeah, I'm sorry about that. I got into that habit hanging around those people. I think I do it because I never want to forget how far I've come since I left the life. My shrink says it's not a problem as long as all I do is talk about it. She calls it an *appropriate defense mechanism*."

I raised an eyebrow when he referenced therapy. But the microwave beeped before I could formulate a question and I decided not to try to look under that particular carpet. Josie served us, and we started eating with a vengeance. Chef Claire's ziti was always better the second day, and, judging by the way we were cleaning our plates, I didn't like the ziti's chances of surviving for a third.

"I meant to ask you guys," Rocco said. "How was your dinner with Lou and his gang the other night?"

I glanced across the island at Josie who paused eating long enough to shake her head.

"How do you know we had dinner with Lou?" I said.

"It's a small town," Rocco said, shrugging as he reached for the bowl of salad.

"Dinner was fine," I said. "Lou's a piece of work, but he seems to be a straight shooter."

Rocco chuckled through a mouthful of Romaine.

"I didn't mean it that way," I said. "But I imagine he's pretty good with a gun."

"He is."

"But that guy Whispers made me nervous," I said.

"Yeah, Whispers tends to have that effect on most people."

"What's the deal with him anyway?" Josie said. "I couldn't understand a word he said all night."

"Well, Whispers made a decision years ago to keep his mouth shut as much as possible," Rocco said, refilling our iced teas.

"Does he have some sort of speech impediment he's embarrassed about?" Josie said.

"Yeah, he had a temporary one a while back," Rocco said. "But he made a full recovery."

"What happened to him?" Josie said.

"Nail gun in the tongue," Rocco said, spearing a forkful of ziti.

"Should I ask?" I said to Rocco.

"No, you shouldn't," Josie said.

I decided that the mental picture was enough and refocused on my lunch. Two bites later, another thought popped into my head.

"Lou said that he wasn't sure that Calducci's or Fatal Franny's murder had anything to do with people fighting for control of his operation," I said.

"Lou's a smart guy," Rocco said.

"So, you agree with him?" I said.

"At first, I wasn't sure. But, yeah, I think I do."

"Are you saying you know who killed them?" I whispered, my eyes wide.

"No, I didn't say that at all," Rocco said. "Why are you always jumping to conclusions like that?"

"Because if she didn't," Josie said. "She'd never get any exercise."

"Funny."

But it was. And I was forced to endure a long round of laughter.

"But to answer your question, Suzy, yes, I have my suspicions," Rocco said, helping himself to some more salad.

"Would you care to share your ideas?" I said.

"No. As far as I'm concerned, there's only one important fact when it comes to the question of who killed Calducci and Franny."

"And what would that be?" I said, leaning forward.

"It wasn't me," Rocco said, beaming at both of us.

Josie snorted.

"I'm going to miss you, Rocco," she said, patting him on the forearm. "When are you heading back home, anyway?"

"Actually, that's something I need to discuss with you," he said, putting down his fork and wiping his mouth. "The lease on my place is up, and I've been thinking about making a change. I like it up here."

"Okay," I said, having no idea where the conversation was about to go.

"And I was talking with Chef Claire the other night, and she mentioned that she'd just fired one of your bartenders."

"Yeah, he was apparently confused about who actually owned the money that was going into the cash register," I said.

"Funny how some people think, huh?" Rocco said. "When she mentioned that you were looking for a new bartender, I offered my services."

His comment caught me by surprise, and I wasn't quite sure how I felt about the idea of a former mobster working behind our bar, but I was willing to hear him out. Josie seemed to be torn about the idea as well.

"You're a bartender?" Josie said.

"I'm a lot of things," he said. "But I'm a very good bartender. And there are rarely any problems in my bar when I'm working. I started tending several years ago after I got out of my previous line of work."

"I thought that was when you started working construction," I said.

"It was," Rocco said. "But I needed a second job to help pay for my therapy sessions. My shrink is really good, but she isn't cheap."

I waited for him to laugh, or even smile, but he was deadly serious.

"What did Chef Claire have to say?" I said.

"She seemed okay with it, but she wanted me to run it by you guys first."

"Well, we trust Chef Claire's judgment and have a hard time saying no to her," I said, glancing at Josie.

"And we'd have an even harder time saying no to someone like you, Rocco," Josie said, laughing.

Rocco laughed along, and I had to admit that, over the past week, we'd both gotten very comfortable having him around. And it certainly couldn't hurt having someone with his skill set working with us, especially late at night when the occasional bar patron decided to turn rowdy.

"I know it might seem a bit strange, and you have every right to be a bit nervous about saying yes, but I want you to run a complete background check on me. You'll see a couple B&E's from about twenty years ago, but nothing since then. Not even a speeding ticket."

I looked at him and decided that this was probably as vulnerable as he let himself get in public. I looked at Josie, who nodded at me.

"Okay, Rocco," I said, smiling at him. "Welcome aboard."

"Thanks, guys. You won't regret it. And I promise I'm going to take very good care of you."

"Well, Rocco, since you're now officially part of the family, do you feel like telling us who you think killed Calducci and Franny?" I said.

Rocco shook his head and glanced at Josie.

"Does she ever take a day off from this stuff?" he said.

"No, I'm afraid she's terminal," Josie said.

"Sorry, Suzy. I'm not ready to do that yet. But when I am, you'll be the first to know."

"I guess I can wait."

"Don't worry," Rocco said. "It won't be long."

Chapter 23

Summer had arrived in Clay Bay, although as far as the annual calendar went, it wouldn't officially start for another week. But school was out, the weather was great, and a wide variety of seasonal businesses on both sides of the River were busy. Thankfully, one person wasn't, and we found Freddie, our local medical examiner, relaxing in his office and enjoying the fact that he hadn't received one of the dreaded phone calls in several days.

Freddie was sitting at his desk organizing various papers and evidence bags into piles when we came in, and he smiled at us, obviously grateful for the diversion from the mundane. He gestured for us to sit down, then nodded at the box of Paterson's doughnuts sitting on his desk that Josie had already spied.

"Good morning, guys," he said, leaning back in his chair and putting his feet up on the desk. "How have you been? I haven't seen you in a while."

"We're good, Freddie," Josie said, eyeing the remaining selection of doughnuts before settling on a chocolate cruller. "Thanks for the doughnut."

"Knock yourself out. They're all yours. My limit is three."

"Amateur," Josie said.

"Well, since no one has died recently," Freddie said. "I doubt if you're here to snoop. So, am I correct assuming that this is a social call?"

"Yes," I said, waving away the box of doughnuts Josie was offering. "Chef Claire's birthday party."

"What about it?" Freddie said. "Tomorrow night at the restaurant, right?"

"Yes, but we've decided to do presents at eight o'clock," I said.

"Okay, that's fine with me," he said, shrugging.

I glanced at Josie and nodded for her to get the ball rolling. We'd debated all morning about which one of us would take the lead on what possibly could end up being a difficult conversation. In the end, we'd flipped a coin. Josie lost.

"And we wanted to give you the option of maybe giving Chef Claire her present earlier," Josie said. "Or even later in the evening when the two of you had some time to be alone."

"After everyone else has gone home," I blurted. "You know, in case you wanted it to be a special moment just between you and Chef Claire."

"No," Freddie said, shaking his head. "I think I'd like to do it in front of everyone. You know, surprise her in front of all of our friends."

"Geez," Josie said, scrunching up her face. "Do you think that's a good idea? Chef Claire hates being the center of attention, and we don't want her to feel embarrassed."

"Why would she be embarrassed? It's her birthday, and a lot of people are going to be giving her presents. Isn't that the way it usually works?"

"Yes, but you've said that your gift is going to be a very special one," Josie said.

"It is," Freddie said, smiling. "And it's something she'll remember forever. I'm going to pick it up tomorrow morning. I had to wait until it was ready."

I looked at Josie, and both of us seemed at a loss for words. Since that was such a rare occurrence, I wasn't sure how to proceed. Our recent conversations with both Freddie and Jackson had convinced us that they were both going to give Chef Claire an engagement ring to match the identical diamond tennis bracelet both of them had given her last Christmas. For some reason, they were both on the same wavelength when it came to deciding what to give her. Unfortunately, for them, they were also both oblivious to the fact that while Chef Claire loved both of them as friends, despite their best efforts, she wasn't *in love* with either of them.

But both Freddie and Jackson had made their frustrations clear when it came to the amount of time Chef Claire was taking to make her choice between them. And while it was apparent to everyone who'd been watching the situation play itself out over the past several months, Freddie and Jackson remained convinced that Chef Claire's choice would ultimately be one of them over the other. The possibility that Chef Claire's decision would be to say no to both of them never seemed to cross their minds.

This year, Chef Claire's birthday should be a memorable one and highlighted by being surrounded by dozens of friends celebrating the opening of her new restaurant. While we understood Freddie and Jackson's impatience and tenaciousness, trying to force Chef Claire's hand by proposing in a public setting seemed insensitive, even selfish. And while we were certain we wouldn't be able to stop either one of them from proposing, our plan was to do everything possible to prevent it from happening in front of a hundred people. Freddie and Jackson would undoubtedly be embarrassed by her public rejection, but Chef Claire could be devastated from being put in that position in the first place. Our hope was that we could gently suggest that they both gave their birthday presents to her in a private setting.

Still searching for something to say, I changed my mind and grabbed a doughnut.

"Can you give us another hint about what you're getting her, Freddie?" Josie said.

I nodded at her. Good job. When in doubt, ask a question.

"No," he said. "I want it to be a surprise. Again, all I'll say is that it is life altering."

"What have you done, Freddie?" I whispered.

"As I told you earlier, I decided to just roll the dice," Freddie said.

"Is it going to make her mad?" Josie said. "Or worse, unhappy?"

"I can't imagine why it would," he said, confused by the question. "And I'd be really surprised if it did either of those things."

I paused to reflect on the exquisite blindness of unrequited love, came up short, then settled for wondering just how dumb two guys could be.

"But if she doesn't like it, that will tell me all I need to know," Freddie continued. "I'll know right away if I've hit a home run, or if I've stepped over the line."

"I guess it's important to try to use moments like that as a learning opportunity," Josie whispered.

"What?"

"Nothing."

"And if Chef Claire doesn't like it, I'm sure I'll be able to find someone else to give it to," Freddie said.

Josie and I stared at each other. Befuddled is probably the best word to describe our expressions.

"Find someone else to give it to?" I said.

"Yeah," he said, shrugging. "It might take some time, but eventually I'm sure someone else would love to have it."

"What is wrong with you?"

"What are you talking about?" Freddie said, officially joining the ranks of the befuddled.

"Haven't you learned anything about how to build a relationship?" I said.

"Really, Suzy? *You're* giving me relationship advice?"

If he didn't have me on the ropes, I would have smacked the smug look right off his face.

"Good point," I said. "Never mind."

"Look, try and understand. I've been trying to get Chef Claire to make up her mind about me for months, and the only thing I've learned is that everything I've done up to this point has been wrong. So, I decided to try something different. What have I got to lose?"

Apart from his dignity and possibly the friendship of Chef Claire's and several other people, not much I decided. But I kept quiet and finished my doughnut.

"I guess it's hard to argue with your logic, Freddie," Josie said. "Just promise us you'll be gentle and play nice."

"Geez, thanks for stopping by, guys," he said, shaking his head. "Why don't you just go ahead and do a cavity search when you're done screwing around with my head? And here I was actually missing you."

Ready for a new topic, I glanced around at the items on Freddie desk and spotted something that looked interesting. At a minimum, it would be something different to talk about.

"Is that the evidence from Calducci's houseboat?" I said.

"Yeah, I'm just trying to get it all organized before I file it away," he said, removing his feet from the desk and sitting back in his chair.

"So, what's the official cause of death going to be listed as?" I said, scanning the various clear plastic bags scattered across the desk.

"Officially, it's going to be categorized as an accidental overdose," Freddie said, warily.

"Not a suicide or maybe a murder?"

"I thought my answer was perfectly clear, Suzy."

"There's no need to get snarky, Freddie."

"Look, Suzy. Calducci's death was suspicious, and we both know it. But there's nothing that suggests suicide. Or even a smidgen of evidence that indicates he was murdered."

"Smidgen? I just love it when you break out the technical terms, Freddie," Josie said, laughing.

"You mind if I have a look?" I said.

"Knock yourself out," he said, gesturing at the desk. "Just don't open any of the bags."

I picked up one of the bags that contained some of Calducci's clothing. Apart from a few food stains, there didn't appear to anything of note on either his shirt or the pair of shorts he'd been wearing. Another bag contained his personal effects including a very expensive watch and a couple of elaborate gold rings set with gemstones.

"Doesn't his widow want these?" I said, holding up the bag containing the jewelry.

"Nope, she stopped by with Jackson for a final wrap up, and she said she doesn't want anything to do with it. I'd like to sell it and donating the proceeds to charity, but I don't think I'll get approval from the authorities yet."

"Because it's considered evidence, right?" I said.

"No," he said, evenly. "Because it's just too early, and there are time statutes that need to be met."

"Sure, sure," I said, nodding. "That watch is worth more than my car."

"The plastic bag is worth more than your car, Freddie said, laughing. "When are you going to get around to getting a new one?"

"As soon as the one I have wears out. It's about to hit 300,000 miles. And I love milestones. Besides, that SUV is like an old friend."

"Oh, so you like to harangue your car on a regular basis, too, huh?"

Josie snorted as she picked her way through the remaining doughnuts.

"Funny," I said, refocusing on the pile of evidence.

I picked up another bag that contained several bottles of prescription drugs. I shook the bag and noticed that most of the bottles were almost empty.

"Man, he sure did take a lot of pills," I said.

"Yeah, he must have been walking around zonked most of the time," Freddie said, nodding. "Of course, we weren't able to determine what his normal levels were given the circumstances."

"Zonked? There you go getting technical again," Josie said, laughing.

"It kind of says it all, don't you think?" Freddie said. "He had high levels of Vicodin, Percocet, and every other pain killer available on the market. As well as a few that aren't."

"Really? Street drugs?" I said.

"No, not really. I wouldn't call them street drugs, although I'm sure you can find them out there if you look hard enough. They're high-end pharmaceuticals you don't see a lot of. And he was also taking blood pressure medicine and a few other things for some stomach problems that showed up on his medical records."

I picked up the bag again and looked at the labels through the clear plastic. Most were from a pharmacy that was obviously near Calducci's home in Rochester, a few others were from local pharmacies, including Howard's. I put the bag down and sat back in my chair.

"Are you satisfied, Miss Marple?" he said.

"Miss Marples," I said, correcting him.

"No, it's Miss Marple," he said. "Both of you always get that wrong. It's singular."

"Really?" I said, glancing at Josie.

"No, that can't be right," Josie said.

"Look it up," Freddie said. "It'll give you something to do other than bug me."

"We didn't mean to upset you, Freddie," I said.

"I know," he said. "You just seem to have a knack for it."

"Well, on that note," I said, getting up from my chair. "I guess we should get going."

"I'll see you tomorrow night," Freddie said. "Chef Claire will be opening presents at eight, right?"

"Are you sure you don't want to give her your gift after the party?" Josie said. "You know, make her wait. Go for maximum impact and all that?"

"I'm positive."

"Yeah," Josie said, heading for the door. "That's what I thought you'd say."

Outside, we stood next to my SUV, and I felt the warm sun beating down on me.

"Too bad we're so busy today," I said. "Great day to be out on the River."

"The first batch of rescues is being delivered this afternoon," Josie said. "I'm afraid it's all hands on deck all day."

"Yeah, but maybe we can work in a short ride before sunset," I said. "I need to clear my head."

"Well, before you try to do that, I suggest you wait until we have our other conversation," Josie said, climbing in the passenger seat. "No sense doing double work."

"Yeah, Jackson. I almost forgot."

"Think it will go any better than the one with Freddie?"

"I doubt it," I said, starting the car.

"Two wedding proposals in the same night," Josie said. "How is that even possible?"

"She was just trying to be nice and not hurt their feelings."

"Probably a bad strategy on her part," Josie said.

"Yup."

"How do you think she's going to play it?"

"I have no idea."

"How would you handle it?"

"I'd probably run away and hide in the walk-in cooler."

"Better than that sub-zero freezer, right?" Josie said, laughing.

"Without a doubt. At least in the walk-in, I could try to eat my problems away," I said. "What would you do?"

"I think I'd probably hit the bar and then go from there."

Chapter 24

Last night, as I was pondering the question of how Jackson and Freddie would handle Chef Claire's birthday and how she might react, another thought had popped into my head. At first, I thought it was just one of those passing notions that seemed to appear out of nowhere, hung around for a while, then faded. And the first time it flashed through my head, I had actually laughed at how absurd it sounded. But the notion had stayed with me and blossomed into a series of what-if questions. Now it nagged at me and threatened to overwhelm my entire thought process. And since it still seemed like such an absurd idea, I decided I would keep it to myself for now and not discuss it with those closest to me.

But keeping it to myself, while undoubtedly giving Josie and my mom a well-deserved respite from my usual rants and rambles, had given me a headache. Whatever had caused this particular idea to pop to the surface from my subconscious hadn't done me any favors, and I decided to do what I always did when I needed to settle down and put things back into some sort of perspective. I headed down to the Inn for an extended visit with our four-legged residents.

I found Josie in the condo area putting Oslo through his daily paces. She had designed a series of activities for him that involved play and learning. As such, Oslo had recently learned to identify and retrieve a dozen different objects by name. This morning's object was a toy elephant that Oslo was holding in his mouth by the trunk and playing keep away with. Josie was doing her best not to laugh but failing miserably.

"Good morning," I said, rubbing Oslo's head.

"Hey, what are you doing here? I thought you were going to try to sleep in," Josie said as she continued to study the dog's movements closely.

"Yeah, I was. But I was awake, so I figured I'd come down and play with the dogs for a while," I said.

"Uh-oh," Josie said, chuckling. "Suzy's got something on her mind. Want to talk about it?"

"No, not yet," I said, deciding to change the subject. "Did you do another round of x-rays on him yet?"

"I did, and they look great. At some point, I'd like to do another MRI, but I don't want to put him under sedation again just yet."

I removed the dog's chart that was hanging on the side of the condo and took a look at it.

"He's gained another three pounds," I said. "That's good. And the stitches are out, right?"

"Yeah, he's eating like a horse. Aren't you, Oslo?" she said, hugging the dog and grabbing the toy out of its mouth.

Oslo barked at her to give it back and sat down staring at the elephant in her hand.

"No, I think that's enough for this morning," Josie said, climbing to her feet and tossing the toy in the air.

Oslo snatched it out of mid-air and pranced around in circles, obviously very proud of himself. As I watched, I realized I was already starting to feel a bit better.

"He still gets tired easily, but that should pass soon," Josie said, closing the door to the condo.

She washed her hands in the nearby sink, then studied me closely as she dried them with a fresh towel.

"Are you okay?" she said.

"Yeah, I'm fine. Just a little preoccupied."

"Chef Claire's birthday preoccupied, or is Calducci on your mind?"

"This morning it's pretty much all Calducci," I said.

"That's what I figured. Do yourself a favor and try not to obsess, okay?"

"Too late," I said. "I was thinking about heading down to the restaurant for a late lunch. You want to come along? Maybe around two?"

"I'd love to, but I'm booked solid all day. And I have a spaying scheduled for three. Say hi to Chef Claire for me. I haven't seen her in three days."

"She's working way too many hours," I said.

"It'll settle down," Josie said. "And she's still in her honeymoon phase. Once the newness of the place wears off, she'll figure out a way to cut back a bit."

"You're probably right," I said. "We went through the same thing the first year we opened."

"Yup," she said. "Okay, I'm off to give some shots to a gorgeous Springer Spaniel. Want to tag along?"

"No, I'm going to see how our new guests are settling in," I said. "I'll catch you later."

I headed off to our new section of the Inn. I found Sammy finishing up the morning feeding of the two dozen dogs who'd recently arrived. If this collection of strays and rescues didn't take my mind off my latest obsession, nothing would.

"Hey, Suzy," Sammy said. "I was just about to let them all out for their morning run."

Sammy pushed the button that opened all the condo doors that led outside to the two-acre play area. Several dogs trotted outside immediately. Others continued to lie around their condo, relaxing.

"Are they all getting settled in?" I said.

"They're doing good," Sammy said. "Josie checked them all out yesterday and didn't find anything major. It looks like the shelter that had them before they got here took good care of them."

"Yeah, they do good work," I said, entering the condo of a beagle that was staring up at me with sad eyes. "They just don't have the resources to keep them indefinitely."

"I can't imagine putting any dog to sleep," Sammy said, turning on the system that automatically refilled each dog's water bowl. "That would be a heartbreaker."

"Yeah," I said, absentmindedly scratching one of the beagle's ears.

"Are you okay, Suzy?"

"I'm fine. You go ahead and get on with the rest of your day, Sammy. I'm going to hang out here for a while. But I'll make sure I close the outside doors before I leave."

"Thanks," he said, giving me a small wave and a curious look as he headed back inside toward the reception area.

I spent about ten minutes with each dog and didn't pay any attention to the time. When I did happen to glance at my watch four hours later, I was surprised by what time it was as well as by how much better I felt. But the thought rolling around my head simply refused to leave. I took a final look around at the new section of the Inn, made sure all the dogs were safe and sound, then got in my car and headed for C's.

The restaurant was in its normal lull between lunch and dinner, and the dining room and bar area were empty. But the kitchen was buzzing as various staff members went about the business of getting ready for that night. I found Chef Claire in the walk-in cooler checking her inventory levels.

"Hey, stranger," I said, glancing around at the wide variety of items on the shelves.

"Hi, Suzy. Did you stop by to have some lunch?"

"I did," I said. "But I'm actually not feeling very hungry at the moment."

"Are you sick?"

I laughed.

"No, I'm not sick. Can't a girl just feel like not eating?"

"Sure, they can," Chef Claire said. "It's just that you never do."

"Funny. Are you ready for your birthday party?"

"Sure. The only thing I have to do is show up, right? I think I can handle that."

"That's all you need to do," I said. "Your staff is going to handle all the food, and Josie and I will take care of everything else."

"Thanks again for doing this. I'm looking forward to it," Chef Claire said. "Well, most of it anyway."

"You're worried about what Jackson and Freddie might do, aren't you?"

"Yeah, a little," she said. "I've been putting off the conversation I need to have with both of them. And I think I might have waited a bit too long."

"Maybe they'll surprise you," I said, then felt the need to amend my comment. "Surprise you in a good way I mean."

"You mean maybe they'll surprise me by not doing anything crazy?"

"Yeah."

"I've been stressing about it way too much. And I finally decided that I have no control over what they decide to do. The only thing I can control is how I react."

"Any idea about what they're going to give you?" I said.

"I have my suspicions. And I'm afraid it could be more jewelry. Jewelry of a highly personal nature that will demand a very serious response neither one of them is going to like hearing."

"Yes, that's what Josie and I are afraid of as well. But we're holding out hope that they won't do anything that stupid."

"For their sake and mine, I sure hope not. A tennis bracelet is one thing, that's something else altogether."

"I think both of them might be trying to force your hand," I said.

"Well, that'll do it," Chef Claire said, leading the way out of the walk-in. "They've both been trying to be cryptic and clever about it. Freddie's been talking about how life-altering his gift is going to be. And Jackson's been prattling on about how it's something that every woman should want. Or need. Or some crap like that. At first, I thought it was cute, but it's started to annoy me."

"Yeah, I get that," I said, nodding. "They both have a tendency to revert to little boys at times."

"Do you think being annoyed by it makes me a bad person?"

"No, I don't."

"Ever since we opened the restaurant, I feel like I've become completely self-absorbed," Chef Claire said, checking one of the ovens. "And I feel terrible because they're both so good to me, and I care about both of them so much."

"But not enough to do that," I said.

"No. That's the one thing I'm sure about."

"Then you need to tell them that," I said.

"I know," Chef Claire said, closing the oven door a bit harder than she probably intended.

Deciding that both of us would benefit from a new topic, I switched gears.

"How's Rocco working out?"

"He's doing great," Chef Claire said. "He's a really good bartender. And I don't think anybody is going to get out of control when he's working the bar."

"Sure, sure," I said, glancing around the kitchen.

"What's the matter, Suzy? You seem preoccupied."

"Yeah. I guess I am. But it'll pass.

"I'm sure it will," Chef Claire said, chuckling. "Just as soon as you figure out if you're right about whatever is bugging you."

"Let's hope so," I said. "I know you're busy so I'm going to get out of your hair."

"I'll bring some goodies home later. Maybe that will make you feel better."

"It couldn't hurt," I said, waving as I left the kitchen.

I wandered into the empty bar and found Rocco organizing his bar stations. He glanced up when he heard me coming.

"Hey, Suzy. What's up?"

"Hi, Rocco. Is everything okay?"

"It couldn't be better. I love this place. What brings you here in the middle of the day?"

"Actually, Rocco, I wanted to talk to you."

"Really?" he said, without glancing up from the lemons and limes he was cutting into quarters. "Should I try to guess what the topic is?"

"The other day you said something that has stayed with me," I said.

"What was that?"

"You said it wouldn't be long before I figured out some things about what happened to Calducci," I said.

"I did say that, didn't I? And have you?"

"I think I might have," I said as tears started to well in my eyes. "And I have no idea about what I should do."

Rocco glanced at me, then put his knife down and wiped his hands with a hand towel. He walked around to the other side of the bar and sat down on the stool next to me.

"Talk to me," he said.

"I've been thinking about all the people who are connected in some way to Calducci."

"Okay."

"And they've all been associated with him for a very long time," I said. "Well, at least they were."

"Yeah, Jimmy, despite all his flaws, and there were a lot of them, tended to be pretty loyal to the people around him."

"And Franny was basically his second in command, right?" I said, dabbing my eyes with a napkin.

"Pretty much. Over the past couple of years, as they got closer, Franny was definitely the first person he went to for advice or when he needed something done. And she was in line to take over should anything ever happen to Jimmy."

"And Lou and his gang had pretty much adjusted to having her around in that role, right?"

"Yeah. They didn't like it at first, but they got used to having to deal with her. And that's what Jimmy wanted, so they figured out a way to make it work."

"So, the loyalty factor went both ways?" I said.

"Absolutely," Rocco said, staring at me.

"That's what I thought."

He continued to stare at me, then a small smile appeared on his face. Eventually, I had to ask him about it.

"What?" I said. "Did I say something funny?"

"No, I was sitting here marveling at what a smart woman you are."

"I sure don't feel very smart at the moment," I said, exhaling loudly.

"You should. Because what you're feeling right now is confusion about what to do next," Rocco said. "Nobody, apart from you and me, has put two and two together."

"It just doesn't seem possible," I said, shaking my head.

"Suzy, if my previous time in that life taught me anything, it's that when money and power are on the table, anything is possible. And anyone is capable of doing pretty much anything."

"But what if I'm wrong?"

"You're not," Rocco said. "Although it seems impossible for you to believe at the moment, it's the only thing that makes any real sense."

"What am I going to do about it?" I said, hearing a tinge of desperation creeping into my voice.

"That's something you're going to have to figure out," he said. "But I promise you I'll be around to make sure nothing happens to you."

"How can people continue to be such a disappointment?"

"Well, I'm just used to it," Rocco said. "But you're still comparing people to all your dogs. And people don't stand a chance when you do that, right?"

I nodded and smiled at him.

"No, they don't," I said. "Thanks, Rocco."

"Anytime. I owe you. And be sure you let me know when you're gonna need me around."

"I will. And I doubt if you'll have to wait very long," I said, climbing down from my stool.

"I'd be surprised if I did."

"Thanks, Rocco. I'll see you at the party."

I headed outside to my car, found the solitary nature of the drive strangely comforting, and took the long way home.

Chapter 25

I found Josie in the living room napping on a couch with Captain tucked under one arm, and Chloe nestled up against her other. All three were snoring softly, and I did my best not to disturb them, but Captain heard me and stirred. And when a hundred pound Newfie stirs, it pretty much gets everyone else's attention. Chloe thumped her tail against the couch, then hopped down and was soon occupying my lap. I rubbed her head and sat waiting there quietly waiting for Josie, who was still wearing her scrubs, to wake up. Eventually, she sat up and blinked and yawned as she looked around the living room.

"Hey. How long have I been out?" Josie said.

"Probably a couple of hours," I said.

"How are we doing on time?"

"We're fine. Chef Claire is still in the shower. What are you going to wear tonight?"

"Probably these," Josie said, laughing as she glanced down at her scrubs. "I don't think I have the energy to shower and change. I'm beat."

"You've been hitting it hard the past few days," I said. "And now that we've expanded, I think we're going to have to hire at least a couple more techs."

"Yeah, I think that's in the cards," Josie said, climbing to her feet and arching her back. "You know, maybe a shower will help."

She headed off with Captain trailing close behind, and she passed Chef Claire in the doorway heading for the living room. Chef Claire had decided on summer casual and looked very comfortable in a pair of shorts and a loose-fitting blouse. She poured herself a glass of wine and topped mine off, spent a few moments rubbing Chloe's belly, then sat down in an overstuffed chair.

"Good call on the outfit," I said. "You look great."

"Thanks," she said, sipping her wine. "It's the first time I've had to think about what to wear in a long time. And I've got a night off. Miracles do happen, huh?"

"Any regrets?"

"Not a one," she said, shaking her head and smiling. "I love that restaurant, Suzy. And I'll never be able to thank you enough."

"Forget it," I said, taking a sip of my wine. "And happy birthday."

"Thanks," she said, raising her glass in a toast.

Captain lumbered back into the living room and climbed up on the couch next to me.

"What happened, Captain? Did your mama kick you out of the bathroom?" I said, giving him a soft thump on the back.

The dog snorted and wagged his tail as he kept a close eye on Chef Claire sitting a few feet away.

"He's amazing," Chef Claire said, staring at the massive Newfie.

"Yeah, he's a good one," I said, rubbing his head.

"I've been thinking about it, and I've decided I'd like to get a dog," Chef Claire said. "A puppy. I've never had one. Do you have any down at the Inn at the moment?"

"No, we don't have a single puppy at the moment, but I'm sure it won't be long," I said. "What made you finally decide to get a dog?"

"I think it was just the cumulative effect of being around you and Josie all these months. I wouldn't have thought two people could be in such a good mood most of the time. And I figure it has to be the dogs. It certainly can't be your charming personalities," Chef Claire said, laughing.

"Funny," I said. "What kind of dog do you want to get?"

"A big one. I've always wanted a big dog. And since I'm living on the River, one that likes the water."

"I'm sure we'll be able to take care of that," I said. "If you like, I can make a few calls."

"That would be great. Thanks."

Josie entered wearing a ragged tee shirt and a pair of cutoff sweatpants. Her hair was wet, and she was rubbing her head vigorously with a towel. She stood in the center of the room with

229

a frown on her face. Then she snapped her fingers and headed back out of the living room.

"How does she do it?" Chef Claire whispered.

"What? Look that good with absolutely no effort?"

"Yeah. I don't get it. And it sure isn't fair."

"Well, you've seen her eat, so it has to be genetics," I said, finishing my wine.

A few minutes later, Josie entered running a comb through her hair. She was now wearing shorts and a silk blouse I'd given her for Christmas. She slipped on a pair of sandals and sat down. Captain hopped down off the couch and bounded up on the other and plopped down on Josie's lap. She rubbed his head, thumped his back, then settled in. I studied Chef Claire as she watched Josie and Captain's well-practiced routine play out with a big smile on her face.

Yes, Chef Claire was definitely dog-ready.

"Are we ready to do this?" Josie said, glancing over at me.

"Let's do it."

I got off the couch and walked across the living room and removed two wrapped presents from the armoire. On my way back to the couch, I handed both gifts to Chef Claire.

"We thought we'd just give you our gift now before the party," I said, sitting back down.

"Oh, guys, you didn't need to do that," Chef Claire said.

"Stop," Josie said, waving it off. "Happy birthday." Then she looked at me. "Should we sing?"

"Oh, let's not," I said. "We'll save that for the party."

"Good call," Josie said. "That way, nobody will be able to pick out the two women with the terrible singing voices."

Not only can't Josie and I carry a tune; we can't even lift one.

"The bigger one is from my Mom," I said. "She wouldn't let us see it, but she did say that it will go perfectly with what we got you."

"I love birthdays," Chef Claire said, rubbing her hands together. "Okay, let's see what Mrs. C. has come up with. Nice wrapping."

Chef Claire slowly removed the wrapping, then opened the box. She reached inside then held two pieces of colorful fabric in the air. Both pieces were tiny.

"So am I correct assuming you got me a trip to a nudist colony?" Chef Claire said, laughing. "This has to be the smallest bathing suit I've ever seen."

"It's either that or a couple of pocket squares," Josie said, shaking her head. "Let me see that thing."

Chef Claire handed both pieces of the bathing suit, and Josie turned it over in her hands, then gave it back to Chef Claire. I shook my head at my mother's ongoing ability to surprise me.

"My mother said she got the same thing for you and me," I said to Josie.

"Great. I've always wanted an all over sunburn."

"I'm not sure this suit is appropriate River attire," Chef Claire said, laughing.

"Yeah, if you wear that around here, you'll never get rid of Jackson and Freddie," Josie quipped, then stopped, embarrassed. "Sorry, Chef Claire. That was uncalled for."

"Don't worry about it," she said. "But I'm confused."

"Open the other one," I said, nodding at the long, thin object in her lap.

Chef Claire opened it and studied it closely before beaming back and forth at us.

"Grand Cayman? Are you kidding?" she said, staring at the first-class air ticket.

"Yeah, we're all going for a week just after Christmas," I said. "My mother has been hounding us to visit her at her place down there. She finally wore us down, and we thought you might want to join us. You know, misery loves company and all that."

"I've always wanted to go there," Chef Claire said, getting up to give each of us a hug. "Thank you so much. I can't wait."

"Didn't you just hear me say that my mother is going to be there?" I deadpanned.

"Stop," Chef Claire said, laughing. "It'll be so much fun." Then she frowned. "Am I really going to have to wear this suit on the beach?"

"Yup," I said.

"I'm going to see if I can get away with just wearing mine somewhere more appropriate," Josie said. "Like in the shower. But Mrs. C. has always been pretty adamant that, when we do come for a visit, we, how did she put it, Suzy?"

"Display our natural assets," I said, staring at the bikini and making a silent vow not to eat after Thanksgiving.

"Oh, they'll be on display all right," Chef Claire said, again holding up the suit for another look.

"I'm sure it's another of my mother's matchmaking ploys."

"Undoubtedly," Josie said, nodding.

"You don't really believe that, do you?" Chef Claire said.

"I'll bet you a hundred bucks my mother already has the list of men she's planning on inviting to be there the same week."

"You need to start figuring out who's going to cover the restaurant that week," Josie said.

"That's right," Chef Claire said. "I think I've got a couple of ideas. We'll make it work."

"Speaking of restaurants," I said, getting up off the couch. "We have a party to get to."

"You sure you don't want to change into your birthday suit before we go?" Josie said to Chef Claire, nodding at the bathing suit.

"You're not funny."

"Disagree."

Chapter 26

The party was in full swing by the time we got to the restaurant, and I spent the first twenty minutes saying hello and catching up with several friends. I eventually worked my way to the bar, had a quick word with Rocco, and saw my mother chatting with Howard at the other end of the long mahogany bar. As I approached, she glanced at my choice of outfit, nodded approvingly, and then beamed at me.

"Hello, darling. I'm so glad you're finally starting to listen to my advice."

"Hi, Howard," I said, giving him a small wave. "How are you feeling?"

"Much better, thanks."

I glanced at the bruises on his face that were hard to see, and I decided Howard was probably wearing some form of makeup to conceal them. Then I looked back at my mother.

"Your advice? You lost me, Mom."

"My advice about how important it is to show up fashionably late to events like these," she said, smiling.

"I'm just late, Mom. There's nothing fashionable about it," I said, accepting a glass of champagne off the tray of a server who was making the rounds. "But speaking of fashion, that's quite the bathing suit you got Chef Claire."

"Wait until you see the one I got you, darling."

I frowned, excused myself, and wandered into the main dining room where I spotted Jackson sitting with his parents at one of the tables. Judging by the expressions on their faces, I'd come at a bad time. But Jackson waved me over, and I sat down.

"Hi," I said, giving Jackson a quick hug before turning to his parents. "Thanks for coming. I know that Chef Claire appreciates you being here."

"We wouldn't have missed it," Jackson said, then looked across the table at his parents. "Isn't that right?"

"Absolutely," Jackson's mother whispered.

"Yeah, you wouldn't want to miss this," his father said, evenly. "You never know who might show up."

Jackson's mother shook her head, exhaled loudly, then got up from the table.

"I need to get some fresh air," she said, then walked off.

Jackson's father excused himself, then followed his wife out of the restaurant.

"It probably wasn't a good idea to bring them along," Jackson said, staring after his parents.

"Are they going to get past the thing with Morrie?"

"The thing? Don't you mean her affair?"

"I'm sorry, Jackson. Forget I mentioned it," I said, patting his hand.

"I can't believe they're getting a divorce."

"Really?"

I was stunned by the news. For some reason, I'd just assumed that two people who'd been married as long as Jackson's parents would find a way to get past what had happened.

"They're both leaving Clay Bay," he whispered. "He's talking about Florida. She wants to go live in Europe. Europe. Can you believe that?"

"What's going to happen with the grocery store?"

"It's going to be sold."

"To who?"

"Well, that's the two-million-dollar question on the table at the moment," Jackson said. "Either they'll take one of the offers they already have, or I'm going to buy it."

"You're seriously considering stepping down?" I said, stunned even more by that idea.

"Yes. And as several members of the town council, especially our beloved mayor, feel the need to keep reminding me, perhaps running a grocery store is better suited to my skill set."

"My mother isn't one of them, is she?"

"No, of course not. She's one of my strongest supporters on the council."

"Howard is encouraging you to step down?"

"Absolutely. Although it seems like encouragement is rapidly becoming a mandate. And the sooner, the better as far as he's concerned," Jackson said. "He said he was most disappointed in, how did he put it, my ongoing and consistent inability to get any traction with the various crimes that come across my desk. Especially the murders of Calducci and Fatal Franny. Which he considers two large black marks on our delightful little town."

I let Jackson's anger and cynicism pass without comment and decided on a new topic.

"Do you have Chef Claire's present with you?" I said, glancing around in the hope that I'd see a big box sitting on one of the chairs that contained anything but an engagement ring.

"I left it in the car," he said, managing a smile. "I hope she likes it."

"Well, you hit a home run at Christmas with the tennis bracelet, so you've got a lot of goodwill in the bank in case you whiff on this one."

"I don't think I'm going to whiff at all," Jackson said, frowning at me. "Speaking of which, have you seen Freddie?"

"No, I don't think he's here yet," I said.

"He's probably trying to show me up by giving Chef Claire his present after I go first," Jackson said, cackling. "Boy is he in for a surprise. There's no way he's going to be able to follow mine."

"Don't you think you two have taken this one-upmanship a bit too far?"

"All's fair in love and war, right?" he said, nodding to himself.

"Try to keep that thought in mind later," I whispered.

"What's that?"

"Nothing," I said, glancing at my watch. "Okay, it's showtime."

I headed toward the large table that had several wrapped presents on it. Josie spotted me and wandered over.

"I think we're ready," I said.

"Let's hope this isn't a complete disaster."

I located the handheld microphone, switched it on, and called for everyone's attention. People drifted in from the bar, and soon the assemblage was in a semi-circle in front of the gift table. Chef Claire approached and blushed as she stood between us. She spent several minutes opening gifts, nervously offering her thanks, and rapidly working her way through two glasses of champagne.

Then I caught a glimpse of Jackson waving an arm at me. He was standing at the back of the crowd and obviously ready to give Chef Claire her present. I glanced at Josie and Chef Claire who both shrugged their shoulders at me.

"Here goes nothing," I whispered.

Then I took a deep breath, exhaled, and spoke into the microphone.

"I believe there's someone at the back of the room who has something he'd like to give Chef Claire."

Jackson started working his way through the crowd. Out of the corner of my eye, I saw Freddie on the other side of the crowd also begin to make his way toward the gift table. Both men saw each other just after they had cleared the crowd and everyone stared and murmured when we noticed the identically wrapped objects they were carrying in both arms.

"Are you kidding me?" Josie said.

"Not this again," I said.

"Either we were completely wrong, or they're holding the largest rock any woman has ever gotten," Josie said.

"I think we whiffed on this one," I said, feeling a mixture of embarrassment and relief wash over me.

"Thank goodness," Chef Claire whispered.

Jackson and Freddie slowly made their way toward the gift table and kept glancing back and forth at each other as they approached. They each placed their gift on the floor in front of Chef Claire and continued to stare at each other, bewildered.

"Happy birthday," Jackson said.

"Yeah, happy birthday, Chef Claire," Freddie said.

"What on earth do you think they got her?" Josie whispered.

"I don't have a clue," I whispered back, then realized I was still holding the microphone. "Okay, Chef Claire, go ahead and open them."

The crowd continued to buzz, still intrigued by the identical packages. Chef Claire leaned down and carefully tore the wrapping paper off the top of Jackson's present. Then she literally screamed with delight. She tore the rest of the paper off, then opened the door and removed one of the most gorgeous Golden Retriever puppies I'd ever seen.

"Oh, Jackson," Chef Claire said, gently hugging the puppy. "I can't believe it."

"You think you can't believe it," Freddie said, staring at Jackson. "You got her a puppy?"

"Not just a puppy," Jackson said, beaming with pride. "A Golden that comes from one of the top breeders in the Northeast."

"Yeah, I know," Freddie said. "Vincent Farms."

"How did you know that?" Jackson said.

"Take a wild guess," Freddie said, shaking his head as he gestured for Chef Claire to open his present.

Seconds later, tears were streaming down Chef Claire's face as she cradled both puppies in her arms.

"Unbelievable," Josie whispered.

"From the same litter?" I said, glancing back and forth at Jackson and Freddie.

"So it appears," Jackson said, glaring at Freddie.

"Man, you sure know how to ruin a guy's surprise," Freddie said, returning the glare.

"They're beautiful," Chef Claire said. "I can't believe how thoughtful you both are."

"And oddly operating on the same wavelength," Josie said. "Well, you did say your present would be life-altering."

"And nothing will alter one's life like two of these little guys," I said, laughing.

"A male and a female, right?" Josie said.

Jackson and Freddie nodded, unable to get the blank stare off their face. Chef Claire handed each of us one of the puppies and gave both men long hugs. I felt the softness of the puppy's fur and got a whiff of puppy breath and wanted one immediately.

Or ten of them.

I handed the puppy back to Chef Claire who continued to be overwhelmed by the two furry bundles in her arms. They'd just recognized each other and scrambled around in her arms wanting to play.

"You'll need to come up names," Josie said.

"I know exactly what I'm going to call them," Chef Claire said. "The male is Al. And the female is going to be Dente."

"Al Dente?" I said, laughing. "That's perfect."

"You guys are too much," Josie said, beaming at Jackson and Freddie. "Well done."

Both men were starting to recover from the shock, and Jackson was the first to start laughing. Soon, Freddie joined in.

"I guess great minds think alike," Freddie said, draping an arm over Jackson's shoulder.

"Yeah. You know, that was a heck of a drive getting to that breeder's place," Jackson said, glancing at Chef Claire. "But the look on her face makes it all worthwhile, huh?"

"It certainly does. But let's make a pact to have a chat before we start buying Christmas presents this year."

Chapter 27

The buffet that Chef Claire's staff had put together was outstanding, but I stopped at two plates. I probably could have forced down a third, but it was impossible to play with the two Golden puppies while eating. So I gave Chef Claire a break so she could eat, and I began to happily roll around on the floor with Al and Dente.

The names she'd given them still cracked me up every time I heard them.

Playing with the puppies also gave me a break from the tension at the table that had been building between Jackson and Howard since we sat down. My mother did her best to keep both men on an even keel, but she ended up doing so much refereeing she should have been wearing a striped shirt and holding a whistle. After listening to them bicker for almost two hours, she turned cranky, and both Jackson and Howard just stopped talking altogether. Despite the damper it put on the party, I welcomed their silence.

The crowd had dwindled considerably, and our table was the only one with people still sitting at it. The remaining handful of guests were in the bar area where Rocco was pouring drinks and keeping a close eye on everything going on.

Chef Claire pushed her plate away and again beamed across the table at Freddie and Jackson. Then she bent down and scooped up both puppies in her arms. I got up off the floor, brushed myself off, and sat back down at the table.

"I'm going to say goodbye to the rest of the guests, and then I think I'll take these little guys home," Chef Claire said. "Would one of you mind driving me home? My hands are kind of full."

Freddie and Jackson bolted out of their chairs.

"Sure," Jackson said.

"Of course," Freddie chimed in.

"And we thought the whole romance-dance was about to be over," Josie whispered.

"I know," I whispered back. "What's she going to do now?"

"Between the restaurant and the puppies she won't have five minutes to even think about it for a while," Josie said. "Maybe I'll start working on them about how much Chef Claire wants a new car for Christmas."

"And then you'd get to use the second one, right?" I said, laughing.

"Of course," Josie cackled, then leaned over to accept Chef Claire's hug. "Goodnight. Just remember, they have tiny bladders and will need to go out every couple of hours."

"Reality sets in, huh?" Chef Claire said, gently hugging the puppies to her chest.

"You have no idea," I said, chuckling. "But goodness gracious just look at them. They're gorgeous."

I gently rubbed their heads and waved goodbye to Chef Claire. Jackson and Freddie also followed her out with a quick wave. As soon as they were out of earshot, my mother turned in her chair and glared at Howard.

"What on earth is the matter with you?" she said.

"What?" Howard said.

"It was supposed to be a party, and you decide to turn it into an inquisition. What has gotten into you?"

"I'm just tired of having a chief of police who can't get out of his own way," Howard said. "And just so you aren't surprised when you hear about it, I'm going to bring up his dismissal at the next council meeting. And I think I've got the votes."

"Doesn't the guy have enough to deal with at the moment?" my mother said.

"Hey, we're all dealing with a lot of stuff," Howard said, then drained the rest of his cocktail.

He'd had several, and I noticed his eyes were watery and his speech was beginning to slur.

"Please, folks. Enough." I said to both of them.

"Thank you," Josie said, also annoyed. "I think I might grab one of those brownies for dessert. You want one?"

"No, I'm good," I said, glancing down at my phone.

"What are you doing, dear?" my mother said, nodding at the phone I was now holding.

"I just need to respond to this text," I said, typing a short message before putting the phone down. "There. All done."

My mother, mollified for the moment, sat back in her chair. Her mood was bordering on dark, and the last thing I wanted was to be the one to bear the brunt if she went off. Josie stood and started for the dessert table. She only got a few steps away before I called her back.

"You know, maybe I will have a brownie," I said.

"Good call," Josie said.

"But you know what would make dessert really special?" I said.

Josie thought for a minute.

"Two brownies?"

"No," I said, laughing. "A scoop of mint chocolate chip."

"Oh, yeah. I'm in."

"I'll go take a look to see if there's a tub of it in the freezer," I said, getting up. "Howard, you want to give me a hand?"

"Sure," he said, shrugging.

He followed me into the kitchen. I headed straight for the freezer but paused before I opened the door.

"Are you okay, Howard?" I said, turning around to face him.

"I'm fine. Just a little buzzed."

"I couldn't help but notice that you've been hitting the booze pretty hard lately," I said.

"That's the funny thing about you, Suzy," Howard said, laughing. "You can't seem to help but notice a lot of things."

"Well, I am a bit of snooper," I said, smiling. "And I just can't seem to stop asking questions."

"That's for sure," he said, nodding.

"Yeah," I said, taking a deep breath. "Like the question of whether Calducci was already passed out on his houseboat when you found him or if the two of you had been drinking together most of the afternoon?"

Howard's face flushed, then he forced a smile and turned coy.

"What on earth are you talking about?"

"Howard. I know," I whispered. "I still have a few questions and some loose ends to put together, but I know you killed Calducci."

"Are you drunk?"

"No."

"Then it has to be insanity," he said, barely managing a throaty chuckle.

"Would you like to know how I figured it out?" I said, watching him closely as he began inching his way toward a large set of chef knives that sat near the edge of one of the prep areas.

"Sure. I'll humor you for a while."

"Like everybody else, I was convinced that the person who killed Calducci had to be someone from inside his operation. And I spent hours trying to figure out who had done it. But then I realized something. Everybody inside his organization seemed to like having Jimmy around, and they're all very loyal to him. And nobody really had much to gain if he got taken out. In short, life was pretty good in and around Calducci's world."

"Was it now?" Howard said. "How good was it for Dot?"

"I did think she might have been behind it for a long time," I said, nodding. "But like the rest of them, she has it pretty good. Well, about as good as any raging alcoholic could have it. In his own weird way, Jimmy took care of her. Kept a close eye on her. Made sure she was safe."

"He ruined her life," Howard said.

"Maybe he did. But Dot made her own life choices. And that's something I'm sure you understand better than most of us."

"That's a cheap shot, Suzy," Howard said, his eyes flaring.

"It's not meant to be. It's just a fact. All those years ago, Dot chose Calducci over you."

Howard laughed.

"And that's the reason I supposedly killed Jimmy? Because he stole my girl?"

"No, I'm sure you came to terms with that a long time ago, Howard. You killed Calducci because he wanted a cut of your business."

Howard visibly flinched. He stared hard at me and rubbed his chin. It was clear that whatever he was thinking about doing would be highly unpleasant for me.

"How on earth did you come up with that insane idea?"

"I started to put it together after you lied to me," I said, noticing for the first time just how quiet and empty the normally hectic kitchen was.

"When did I lie to you?"

"It was the afternoon Josie and I stopped by your place. You were taking inventory, and your bruises were still pretty fresh. I asked you about the last time you'd seen Calducci, and you said it had to be several years ago. Remember?"

"Yeah, I remember," he said, raising an eyebrow at me.

"But you'd seen Calducci recently."

"How on earth would you know that?"

"Because he stopped by your pharmacy to get a couple of his prescriptions refilled. I saw the bottles in one of the evidence bags in Freddie's office. The date on the bottles was a couple of days before he died. My guess is that you were chatting, just catching up on old times, and Jimmy told you that he thinking about buying a place up here. Then he probably casually mentioned something about expanding his business interests. What did he want from you, Howard? Twenty percent?"

"Twenty-five," Howard said, snatching one of the large knives off the counter.

I glanced down at the size of the knife he was extending toward my stomach and gulped. I looked around the empty kitchen, blinked into the harsh overhead lighting, then forced myself to relax.

"You staged the robbery at your store, didn't you?"

"Very good, Suzy," he said. "I have to hand it to you. Nobody was even close to figuring it out."

"Jackson would have got there eventually," I said.

"That moron?" he scoffed. "I seriously doubt it."

"Jackson's just been preoccupied lately. It's no excuse for not doing his job better, but I understand it."

"I guess we'll have to agree to disagree. But none of that matters now," he said.

"Probably not. So what happened on the houseboat?" I said.

"It was pretty much like you said. Jimmy had invited everybody out on his houseboat, but most people passed on the offer. By the time I got there, he was alone and passed out below deck. I'd brought along a couple bottles of pills I'd taken during the so-called robbery, and I stuffed them down his throat. Since they were painkillers he already had prescriptions for, I figured there was a good chance the cops and Freddie would classify it as an accidental overdose. And even if they didn't, I'd be the last person they'd be looking for. I forced the pills down, then I got back in my boat and left. It took all of five minutes."

"And you thought that would be the end of it," I said.

"Yes, I did."

I inched my way back toward the freezer door. Howard smiled and took a step closer. The knife remained only a foot away from my midsection.

"But then Fatal Franny surprised you, didn't she?"

"She certainly did. She stopped by the pharmacy and told me that she was taking over and that I would still be on the hook for the twenty-five percent."

"So you decided to play along, and then you laid the charm on her and invited her out on the boat," I said.

"Everybody has to be good at something, Suzy," he said, smiling. "I just happen to be good with women."

"And she was in the process of disrobing at Lover's Cove and had to remove her gun and holster," I said, fishing a bit, but knowing I was on the right track.

"Very good," he said, laughing. "I insisted. I told Franny that we didn't want the gun going off in the middle of...well, you know."

"Yeah, I got it, Howard. And then you grabbed her gun and shot her right between the eyes."

"Yes, I did," he said, his eyes glazing over momentarily as the memory returned. "I'll never forget the look of shock on her face just before I pulled the trigger. I'm still having nightmares about it."

"And that's why you're drinking all day, right?"

"I'm sure that's a big part of it," he said, pausing to give it some serious thought. "Hopefully, it's just a temporary phase I'm going through. But I will say that I have a better understanding why Dot does it. It does help to kill the pain."

"I'm still confused about how you staged the attack and beating," I said, determined to get him to tell the rest of the story.

"I have to give myself a lot of credit for coming up with that," he said. "But you and Josie and your dogs almost ruined that."

"So you were on shore the whole time?" I said, nodding.

"Yeah, after I shot her, I dragged Franny's body into a thick patch of brambles and then settled in next to her. My plan was to wait until dark, and then I heard the two of you stumbling around and hollering my name. At one point, the Newfie actually sniffed us out and was about ten feet away. But the brambles were really thick and had needles all over the place. The dog got his nose into one of them and then decided he had better things to do. I was glad he left. I would have hated shooting you and your dogs."

"Geez, Howard," I said, bewildered by the mess my longtime friend had created. "What were you thinking?"

"Self-preservation. Survival," he said, shrugging. "I've worked too hard to give a chunk of my business away to a couple of lowlifes like Calducci and Franny."

"And you thought that it would eventually settle down and you'd get on with your life."

"Sure. But thanks to you, now I'm going to have to get on with the rest of it somewhere else."

"I'm sorry about that, Howard," I said, shrugging. "But you killed two people."

"Yeah, you seem crushed, Suzy," he said, chuckling.

"And all the heat you were putting on Jackson was part of the plan. You figured that if you came across as indignant and angry that the murders weren't being solved, you'd attract even less attention."

"That partially right. I still think Jackson is an idiot. But a self-righteous mayor outraged by the situation and doing his best to protect the reputation of Clay Bay and the safety of its residents is pretty hard to argue with."

"You're right," I said. "But I can't for the life of me figure out how you made the fake attack work."

"That was brilliant, wasn't it? I have a camp on Wellesley Island I use when I want to get away or have a liaison with somebody who needs to keep it a secret. And I have an old truck I keep there that I rarely drive into town. So the chances that anybody would see the truck and connect me to it were very low. I waited until it got dark, then I carried Franny's body three miles through those woods. It almost killed me. She wasn't a small woman. I spent most of the night recovering from that ordeal, then I wrapped her up in a tarp and tossed her in the back of the truck. When I got to town, I was about to put her body in the trunk of my car I had parked behind the pharmacy. Then I got lucky."

"Morrie the Meat Guy stopped at the gas station right next door to your place. And when he went inside you hung Franny from one of the hooks in the back of his truck," I said, staring at him.

"You are good," Howard said. "Over the years, I've learned that Morrie loves to chat. And he and Charlie always spend at least twenty minutes catching up over a cup of coffee every time Morrie stops by to fill up. It was still dark, so I parked my truck next to Morrie's and put Franny in the back. I remembered seeing it in a movie, and the idea just popped into my head."

"Goodfellas," I said.

"Yeah, that's the one. Great movie," he said, staring off into the distance momentarily before refocusing on me. "Then I drove back to my camp, inflicted a bunch of cuts and bruises on myself, then walked to the road that's about a mile away, laid down by the side of the road, and waited for someone to find me. It took all day before they did, but it was okay. I needed to sleep anyway."

He laughed and glanced down at the knife he was holding. Then he nodded and looked at me.

"So what now, Howard? Are you going to stab me?"

"Not unless I have to, Suzy. I'd hate to have to hurt you. But I think spending a night in that freezer might be the best thing."

"I'd prefer the walk-in," I said.

"I'm sure you would," he said, laughing as he wiggled the knife at me. "But let's go with the sub-zero. It locks from the outside."

"How are you going to explain my disappearance tonight?"

"That's easy," he said. "After I lock you in the freezer, I'm going to walk back out there, and tell Josie and your mother that you didn't feel well and decided to go home."

"Do you think one night in there will kill me?" I said.

"Gee, I hope not," he said. "But in the morning when Chef Claire finds you in there, I'll be long gone."

"Where are you going to go, Howard?"

"Nice try, Suzy. I'm going to miss your ability to stick your nose where it doesn't belong. It's actually quite charming."

"You know, Howard. I'm going to miss you, too."

"Okay, that's enough of a goodbye. Let's get this over with," he said, waving the knife at the freezer door.

I nodded and turned around to open the freezer. I pulled the heavy door wide open and then turned back around to look at Howard. He seemed completely at peace with what he was about to do. So much for our being life-long friends.

"Take care of yourself in there, Suzy," he said, chuckling. "Maybe you should try cuddling up with a stack of those prime ribs."

"That's a great idea."

Howard was startled by the deep voice behind him, and he wheeled around just in time to watch Rocco grab his wrist and snap it like a twig. The knife clattered to the floor, and Rocco kicked it away. Howard screamed in agony, and Rocco literally tossed him into the freezer, then closed and locked the door behind him. We could hear his muffled cries and shouts coming through the thick metal door.

"Did you get all that?" I said, smiling at Rocco.

"Every word," he said. "I thought he'd never shut up."

"I probably could have done better with some of my questions, but that knife was pretty distracting."

"It's a big knife," he said. "But you did great."

"And you kept your promise of being around just in case I needed you."

"Well, after you sent that text, I figured something was up. And then I saw the two of you head to the kitchen. Good decision on your part."

"Thanks, Rocco."

My mother and Josie burst into the kitchen.

"We heard somebody screaming," my mother said.

"Let me guess," Josie said. "We're out of the mint chocolate chip."

"Suzy just solved two murders," Rocco said, beaming at me.

"Calducci and Fatal Franny?" Josie said, wide-eyed.

"Yeah," Rocco said.

"Really? Who is it?" my mother said, glancing around the empty kitchen.

"Howard," I said.

"Howard?" my mother said, frowning as she staggered backward a couple of steps. "No way."

"Yes, Mom."

"Where the heck is he?" Josie said.

"He's in the freezer," Rocco said.

"Was that him screaming?" my mother said.

"Yeah," I said. "I think he hurt his wrist."

Rocco looked down at the floor and stifled a laugh.

"I'm stunned," my mother said, leaning against a counter. "Howard? Why on earth would he do that?"

"Long story, Mom."

"All the good ones are, darling."

"Should we call Jackson?" Josie said.

"Yeah, when we get around to it," I said. "Let's say we wait until Howard gets a good chill going. For now, let's go have dessert, and I'll try to catch you up on things."

"So, no ice cream, right?" Josie said.

I shook my head at her and led all of us back to the dining room.

Then we grabbed a tray of the brownies and decided that the bar was probably a better option.

Epilogue

Jackson appeared to be almost as happy dragging Howard out of the freezer to arrest him as he'd been giving Chef Claire the puppy. We'd let Howard hang out in the sub-zero for a couple of hours before calling Jackson, and after I saw our mayor shivering and clutching himself, I decided that I probably wouldn't have survived a full night in there.

My mother had polished off a couple of glasses of champagne, one more than her usual limit, and she'd worked herself into a frenzy, then taken the opportunity to badger and yell at Howard as soon as Jackson dragged him out of the freezer. Her harangue continued even after Jackson had stuffed him into the back of his police car. While I wasn't surprised by some of the language my mother used, I was taken back a bit by some of the creative word-pairings she'd come up with on the spot.

Two days later, I heard her use a lot of the same language after the Town Council had called an emergency meeting and unanimously elected her to finish out the last two years of Howard's term as mayor. It was a position she had previously held and hated, but she had taken her responsibilities seriously and done a good job. But she'd been miserable the entire time, and I doubted if her second term in office would be any different.

I'd fought back a chuckle when she'd stopped by the house to tell us the news. I congratulated her and immediately started to prepare myself for two years of what I knew would be marked by long periods of extreme crankiness and severe mood swings.

And who knew how my mother would react.

The entire town was in shock after the news about Howard spread like wildfire. For a week, it was the main topic of conversation in every store, bar, and restaurant, our place included. But eventually, things settled down as the season really got rolling, and the summer residents and tourists arrived in droves and helped take our minds off the question of how our longtime friend and mayor could have so quickly gone off the rails.

As for Howard, he was refused bail and is currently sitting in jail awaiting trial and waiting for his broken wrist to mend.

Except for Rocco, the Calducci cast of characters has all left the area to return home, and I imagine sort out how they're going to handle things now that their patriarch is gone. Dot and Pee Wee were still together the last time I saw them. They stopped by for lunch at C's, and Dot was already half-hammered, and Pee Wee was his usual protective self. It seems to be a bizarre relationship, but, given my track record on that front, who am I to judge?

Rocco continues to do a great job behind the bar, and Chef Claire has decided to remain with Josie and me at the house. As such, Rocco was more than happy to accept our offer to rent the vacant apartment above the restaurant that was originally earmarked for Chef Claire. We were also pleased when Rocco expressed his interest in adopting Oslo. Rocco has turned out to be a total dog person, and the two are inseparable.

We were delighted when Chef Claire decided to stay at the house, and dogs now officially outnumber the people living there four to three. But the two Golden puppies are amazing. Al and Dente – the names still crack me up every time I hear them - quickly bonded with both Chloe and Captain and having all four of them in the same room when their energy is up makes them quite the handful. Each night, Chef Claire sleeps with a puppy on either side of her, and she's happy to report that all three of them are sleeping very well. But she still hasn't been able to have the conversation with either Freddie or Jackson, and I'm beginning to wonder if she'll ever find the courage to tell her two good friends thanks, but no thanks. For their part, Freddie and Jackson are still basking in the glow of the total home run they both hit with their birthday presents, and they don't seem too concerned about having that particular conversation.

I guess when you already know the answer, why bother forcing the question?

Jackson's parents are making final arrangements for their pending departure, and the divorce papers have been submitted. Jackson has a huge decision to make and not much time to make it. The choice between being our chief of police or spending the rest of his life running a grocery store is stark. And the only advice I had for him when he asked me the other day what he should do was to find the one thing he loved doing more than anything else and then do it for the rest of his life.

This is an area where I think I have something to offer since I'm doing the one thing I love more than anything. And I certainly don't plan on stopping anytime soon.

Part of that life includes fishing during bass season. The other day I'd gotten a tip from a local fishing guide about a rock shelf near an island about a half-hour boat ride from the Inn. The shelf extends offshore about thirty feet below the water and apparently is a favorite spot for smallmouth as they wait for the deeper sections of the River to warm up a bit. According to the guide, the bass are ravenous early in the morning, but one has to get there before the sun comes up.

And so it came to pass that Josie and I found ourselves catching and releasing bass after bass as the sun slowly came up over the horizon. We'd gotten up so early that even Chloe and Captain had decided to stay home. Chloe had slowly opened one eye when I turned on the bedroom light at five, then had snorted and gone right back to sleep. According to Josie, Captain hadn't even bothered to open his eyes.

I put my fishing rod in its holder and refilled our coffee mugs. I sat down and stretched out and gazed out over the River. I waved to the fishing guide who was about two hundred yards away and his clients for the day seemed to be catching as many fish as we were.

"It's going to be a beautiful day," I said, reaching for a doughnut.

"I'll let you know as soon as I wake up," Josie said, laughing. "Man, it's early. I can't believe I let you talk me into this."

"All I had to say was that we'd be going past Summerman's island," I said, glancing over at her.

"That had nothing to do with it," she said. "You just caught me in a weak moment."

"Sure. Summerman did say he'd be back in the area on the first day of summer, didn't he?"

"Yes, he did."

"And if I'm not mistaken, this is officially the first day of summer, right?" I said.

"It is."

"Then why don't we just swing by his island on our way back and see if he's around?"

"I guess it couldn't hurt," Josie said. "You know, do the neighborly thing and welcome him back."

I laughed. Josie had been waiting for Summerman to get back into town since the time she had met him last fall on the day he was leaving. To say the least, she was smitten.

"I think I'm a bit fished out," Josie said.

"Wow, you are in a hurry to find out if he's around. The sun's barely up."

"No, I've just had enough fishing for one day," she said, lying through her teeth. "And this catch and release still has me wondering at times why we even bother fishing in the first place."

"Because it's fun," I said, beginning to pack both of our rods away. "And it's a life metaphor."

"A life metaphor?" she said, raising an eyebrow. "Do tell."

"Absolutely. It's about the challenge. The struggle to achieve. Striving for success. Overcoming long odds and the elements. For both us and the fish. You can learn a lot about survival just by being out here."

"I'd like to say you're weird, but I'm sitting right here in the boat with you."

"And that would make both of us weird, right?"

"Exactly," Josie said, laughing.

"But the best part of all of it is that nothing has to die in the process," I whispered.

"That would be a nice change," Josie said, nodding. "Okay, let's swing by Summerman's place and say hi."

"He's a rock star, and I doubt if he's even awake yet," I said.

"Then we'll leave him a note," she said, gesturing for me to start the boat. "Let's go."

"Okay, okay," I said, shaking my head. "Keep your pants on."

"I'll do my best," she said, laughing.

I headed in the direction of Summerman's island and waved goodbye to my fishing guide friend on the way past his boat. The island wasn't far, and we were soon able to make out its outline in the early morning sky. I slowed as we left the main channel and headed into the shallower water.

"Why are you slowing down?" Josie said.

"There's a huge shoal that runs off one side of the island, and I'm not exactly sure where it is," I said, scanning the horizon.

Then I noticed two objects moving through the water in the direction of the island.

"What on earth is that?" I said, pointing at the objects.

"It looks like a couple of swimmers," Josie said, reaching for the binoculars. "What do you know? It's Summerman and his dog. What was his name again?"

"Murray," I said, grabbing my own pair of binoculars. "That water still must be freezing. It has to be about eighty feet deep around here."

"Yeah, I sure wouldn't be going in," Josie said. "Wow. What do you know? He's skinny-dipping."

"Really?" I said, lowering my binoculars to glance over at her.

But she didn't even notice because her binoculars were locked on Summerman. I laughed and punched her arm.

"Put those away," I said. "We're getting close."

Josie complied, and I continued to steer the boat toward them. Murray spotted us first, and I heard his distant woof. Moments later, Summerman stopped swimming and began to tread water. Eventually, he recognized us and waved an arm at us. The dog swam in small circles around him, and I realized that it was a protective maneuver on his part. I put the boat in neutral, and Summerman grabbed the side of our boat with one hand as Murray continued to bark and paddle next to him.

"Hey, guys," Summerman said, giving us a strange smile.

"Are you okay?" I said.

"Yeah, I'm fine," he said, blinking several times. "I'm just trying to get used to being back here."

"And you thought an early morning swim in that water would help?" Josie said, laughing.

"Yes, it's pretty cold. Isn't it, Murray?"

The dog woofed but didn't seem to mind the water temperature one bit.

"Do you always start your day this way?" Josie said.

"You mean with a swim?" he said, frowning up at us.

"No. I meant that you're naked, Summerman," Josie said.

"Nothing gets past you, huh?" I whispered.

"Funny."

"Well, let's just say that it's sort of a tradition for Murray and me to start our summer by doing this," he said, casually. "And we do the same thing on the official last day of summer."

"I'll mark my calendar," Josie said.

"Josie," I whispered. "Try to control yourself."

Summerman laughed and rubbed Murray's head with his free hand.

"Well, it's nice to be back," he said. "Hey, why don't the two of you come over for dinner tonight? I have some friends coming in, but they won't be here until tomorrow. I'd hate to eat alone on my first night back, and while I love Murray's company, he's not much of a conversationalist this time of year."

"This time of year?" I said, frowning.

"Forget it," Summerman said. "I'm babbling. Does seven-thirty work for you?"

"Perfect," Josie said.

"No fish, right?" I said.

"No, Suzy. We won't be having fish," Summerman said, laughing. "See you then." Then he looked over at his dog. "I'll race you to shore, Murray."

The dog woofed loudly and took off in a flash. Summerman watched him swim away, and his eyes danced as he stared after the dog.

"Man, he's fast. You think you can catch him with the head start you gave him?" I said, watching the dog work his way through the water.

"No. He always beats me anyway," Summerman said, gently pushing away from the boat. "I'll see you tonight. I'm looking forward to catching up. I can't believe the news about Howard."

We watched him make his way toward the island and laughed when we noticed that Murray had turned around and was waiting for Summerman to catch up.

"What a great dog," I said.

"Yeah."

"Are you okay?" I said, glancing over at Josie who continued to dreamily stare out at the water.

"I'm fine. Why do you ask?"

"Nothing. It's just that you look a little…flushed. Yeah, let's go with flushed."

"Suzy?"

"Yes, Josie," I said, doing my best to stifle a laugh.

"Shut up."

Made in the USA
Middletown, DE
31 March 2022

63426580R00156